TWO NOVELS

# Baby

# Journey

TWO NOVELS

# Baby

# Journey

## Patricia MacLachlan

DELACORTE PRESS

Published by Delacorte Press
an imprint of Random House Children's Books
a division of Random House, Inc.
New York

A writer friend once told me, "I can see the threads of your life in your books." That is true, and looking back, I can see that in my books *Journey* and *Baby* I worked out how I felt about issues in my own life. I often change life in my books so that I can make life turn out the way I want. This is one of the joys of writing books.

*Baby* began when all of my children, John, Jamie, and Emily, went off to college or to live in faraway places. Truthfully, I loved having children and being around them. And suddenly they were gone. The mother in me wished for more children—or at least something to care for. The writer in me wrote *Baby*, a book that fulfilled on paper my wish to have a baby left on my doorstep. I can see my daughter, Emily, there in the voice of Larkin—a strong girl.

*Journey* began with a talk with my son John, a photographer who now lives in Tanzania. We were talking about photographs, mainly portraits.

"When you look through the portrait camera, you see the image upside down," John said.

"Really?"

"Your retina sees things that way, too," he added. "But your brain corrects it."

"Then what's the truth?" I protested.

John liked this. And this led me to *Journey*, a book about family and about the way photographs can sometimes show us the truths we need to know.

My other son, Jamie, is in the book, too. When he was small and didn't want to do something, he protested, like Journey—"But I'm only a little boy!"

Sometimes I think I put bits and pieces of the lives of my children in my books to keep them safe there forever. I hope you will find some piece of your life in these stories, too.

*Patricia MacLachlan*

# CONTENTS

# Baby

*This book is for Jamie MacLachlan.*

*I am not resigned to the shutting away of loving hearts
    in the hard ground.
So it is, and so it will be, for so it has been, time out
    of mind:
Into the darkness they go, the wise and the lovely.
    Crowned
With lilies and with laurel they go; but I am
    not resigned.*

—from "Dirge Without Music"
Edna St. Vincent Millay

# Summer's End

*The memory is this: a blue blanket in a basket that pricks her bare legs, and the world turning over as she tumbles out. A flash of trees, sky, clouds, and the hard driveway of dirt and gravel. Then she is lifted up and up and held tight. Kind faces, she remembers, but that might be the later memory of her imagination. Still, when the memory comes, sometimes many times a night and in the day, the arms that hold her are always safe.*

# Chapter One

In the evenings my father danced. All day long he was quiet and stubborn, the editor of the island newspaper. But in the evenings he danced.

Lalo Baldelli and I sat on the porch swing, clapping our hands over our ears when the six o'clock ferry whistle blew, and inside, as always, my father began to tap-dance on the coffee table. It was a low, tiled table, blue and green Italian marble. My father loved the sound of his taps on the tiles. He danced every evening before dinner, after his six crackers (Ritz) with cheddar cheese (extra sharp), between the first glass of whiskey that made him happy and the second that made him sad. He always began slowly with "Me and My Shadow," then "East Side, West Side," working up to Lalo's favorite, "I Got Rhythm." Wherever he was, Lalo would come to our house before dinner so he wouldn't miss my father's wild and breathless "I Got Rhythm" that finished with a flourish, hands stretched out as if playing to a large audience. Lalo was the only one who applauded, except later, of course, when Sophie did.

There was a rhythm to the rest of my family too. When my father began to dance my mother would come out of her studio, covered with paint if her work was not going well; and Grandma Byrd would come up from her afternoon nap, her hair untouched by sleep.

Today my mother came out onto the porch, carrying a silver bowl that held batter for a cake that would never be baked. She carried spoons for Lalo and me, and the large wooden one for herself.

"You'll like this, Larkin," she said to me, handing me a spoon.

"What kind?" asked Lalo, peering into the bowl.

"Spice," said Mama.

"That's much better before it's baked," said Lalo. Mama smiled at him.

"You bet," she said, taking a huge spoonful, then handing us the bowl.

Mama was covered with flecks and smears of paint, and I could tell by the colors what she was working on. The island. Blue for the water of the island ponds and the sky and the sea; green for the hills—light green for the meadows and fields, dark for the stands of spruce. Mama was a walking landscape. That meant trouble, more paint on Mama than on canvas. That meant she was restless. Mama saw me looking at her clothes.

"I can't concentrate," she said, her voice flat and unhappy.

The porch window behind me opened.

"Are you eating batter?" Byrd asked.

"Spice," said Mama and Lalo at the same time.

The window closed, and we heard Byrd slide open the mahogany pocket doors to her room. She appeared on the porch with her own spoon.

Lalo offered her his seat.

"My dear," she murmured, and sat, holding up her hand in what Mama called her queen's wave.

Byrd grew up in a grand house with pillars and many porches, and could have been a queen. She was seventy years old with white hair piled on her head, and rows of neck wrinkles like necklaces.

Byrd said often that she was pleased to have all her faculties. Once, though, after an island party and some punch, she called them facilities, and some townspeople still believed that she had many bathrooms in the house and that she loved them all. Lately she had discovered fancy stockings. Today they were black with jewels that sparkled as she moved. The jewels worked like little prisms, tossing light around, causing spots to tremble on the porch ceiling.

"Great socks," said Lalo, making Byrd laugh.

"Stockings, Lalo," she corrected him. "One day you may live off island, you know, and you'll see things you never dreamed of. Including patterned stockings."

Lalo looked at Byrd, horrified, his spoon halfway to his mouth.

"Not me," he said. "I'll never leave this island. Everything is here."

Mama smiled wistfully.

"Almost everything," said Byrd. She sighed. "But I do miss—" She stopped suddenly, and I looked at her, waiting for her to say what I knew she missed. What *I* missed.

Mama turned to look at her, too, her eyes sharp and sad at the same time. Then Mama's expression changed as she looked up at Papa, who stood at the doorway, his face all flushed from tap-dancing.

"What?" asked Papa, out of breath. "What do you miss?"

"Something," said Byrd lightly, her tone changing. "I don't know just what, but I miss something."

"I know," said Mama. "I'm restless. Tomorrow the last summer ferry leaves. And then?"

"We get the island back," Papa said, "and everything will be quiet and peaceful and all ours."

"Excitement," said Byrd suddenly, her face bright with memory. "We need something new and exciting to happen."

"Like dinner?" suggested Papa.

"Oh!" Mama jumped up so quickly that the porch swing almost toppled Byrd. "The pot roast is done. Here." She gave the batter bowl to Papa.

"What was this?" he asked, sampling it.

"That was dessert, dear heart," said Byrd. She got up very slowly. Then, with a quick smile and a sudden shake of herself, like a wren, she went inside.

"Such excitement," said Papa softly. Then he looked at us. "This is enough excitement." There was a pause. "Isn't it?" he added, asking himself the question.

We ate dinner as the sun set; candles on the table, the dinner a yearly celebration that tomorrow the island visitors would leave. The seasons on our island rose and fell in a rhythm like the rise and fall of the tides. Autumn was ours with quick colors, leaves flying until they were gone and we could see the shape of the island. The land rose and fell, too, from the north point where the lighthouse stood, curving down into valleys like hands holding pond water.

Soon winter would come, the winds shaking the windows of the house, the sea black. Herring gulls would sit out of the wind on our porch, watching for spring that would come so fast and cold, we would hardly know it was there. Then summer, visitors would come off the ferry again, flooding us, the air heavy with their voices. And again, at summer's end they would be gone like the tide, leaving behind small signs of themselves: a child's pail with a broken handle, a tiny white sock by the water's edge. Bits and pieces of them left like good-byes.

Suddenly, as we ate, a gull flew low over the house, its crazy shriek startling us. We looked up, then at each other. Nervous looks and laughter. But there was nothing to be nervous about on that day.

It was the next day, after the last ferry took the summer people away, that it happened.

# Chapter Two

Puffs of wind came off the water, sending Lalo's hat flying down the beach. He ran after it, small sprays of sand sent up by his feet. A kite whirled and dipped, suddenly plunging into the water. There was a group sigh behind us, summer tourists on the porch of Lalo's parents' hotel. They stood like birds on a line, their bags all packed, faces red, noses peeling from summer sun. Summer's end.

"Lalo!" Mr. Baldelli called from the porch, and we ran up to carry bags to the hotel truck, hoping for tips.

"My umbrella, don't forget, Larkin," called Mrs. Bloom. Mrs. Bloom came every summer, bringing her beach umbrella, her chair, and her little hairy dog whose full name was Craig Walter. I took the yellow umbrella from Mrs. Bloom. In her arms Craig bared his teeth at me.

The Willoughbys clutched handfuls of wild-flowers, almost gone by. Their children lugged suitcases of rocks, dead horseshoe crabs, and sea urchins that would crumble before they got home.

Lalo and I sat on the back of the truck for the short ride along the beach road to the dock. We passed people on bicycles, their baskets filled. We passed parents walking with children, babies in backpacks, dogs loping nose to the ground behind them.

At the dock cars were already lined up waiting to leave. Griffey and his musical group were there, playing "Roll Out the Barrel," the only song they knew. Griffey played accordion and Rollie the fiddle. Arthur played his saxophone, and old man Brick played only three notes on his bagpipe: major, minor, and "something diminished," as Mama put it.

Papa was there saying good-bye to summer people. I could see the stubble on his face, the beginnings of his yearly winter beard that he shaved off every June before the tourists returned. Byrd and Mama were there, too, Byrd's legs sparkling, her hair blown like tossed snow. Mama handed a wrapped package to a woman, then smiled at Lalo and me across the dock because she had sold a painting. A child in overalls ran toward the dock's edge, arms up, until his laughing father caught him up in his arms, swinging him over his head. A young woman holding a baby stood near, watching us. A dogfight began, then ended as owners pulled on their leashes.

The cars, all stuffed with suitcases and sleeping bags and coolers, beach chairs tied on top, began to move onto the ferry. Then the bicycles were wheeled on.

"Good-bye!" called Mrs. Bloom, waving one of Craig's small paws at us.

"Good-bye!" we shouted back.

And the gates were closed with a metal clang, the huge lines tossed on board.

Surprisingly, Griffey, Rollie, Arthur, and old man Brick began a new song.

"Whatever?" exclaimed Mama behind me.

"They've learned something new," cried Lalo.

"What is it?" I asked.

" 'Amazing Grace,' " said Papa, grinning.

The *Island Queen* moved off, and my mother began to laugh. Byrd sang in her old voice:

*Amazing Grace, how sweet the sound,*
*That saved a wretch like me!*
*I once was lost, but now am found;*
*Was blind, but now I see.*

As the boat reached the breakwater we all put our hands to our ears as the whistle blew. Above, the sky was ice-blue, low clouds skimming across, and without the noise like one of Mama's paintings. And then it was quiet, a handful of us left: Griffey and the boys packing up their instruments, Lalo's father hosing down his truck at the dock's edge, islanders walking away. A couple I didn't know held hands. Maybe they would fly out tonight on the small plane. The woman holding the baby still watched us. A cloud slipped in front of the sun.

Summer's end.

"Your mom cried," said Lalo as we walked up from the water through the fields.

"She always cries at the end of summer," I said. "At the end of anything. At weddings." I looked at Lalo. "And parades."

Lalo burst out laughing. The Fourth of July parade was led by Griffey's goat and the sewer-pump truck, and still my mama cried.

Lalo and I sat on the rock by the pond. Water bugs skimmed along the surface; a fish jumped, sending out circle after circle. Way off in the distance the ferry was a small dot, getting smaller, a thread of smoke rising from its stack.

"So," said Lalo. Lalo began most sentences with *so*. Ms. Minifred, the school librarian, was trying to break him of the habit.

"Get to it, Lalo," Ms. Minifred said. "You will miss your own marriage when the minister asks you if you take this woman and you begin with *so*. You will miss the end of your life, too, when you try to leave behind some wondrous words."

Ms. Minifred liked wondrous words. She loved the beginnings of books, and the ends. She loved clauses and adverbial phrases and the descriptions of sunsets and death. Lalo called her "It Was the Worst of Times Minifred."

"You are a full-time job, Lalo," Ms. Minifred told

Lalo once after he had asked her twelve questions in a row.

"Thank you, Ms. Minifred," said Lalo, missing the point.

I wondered what she would do when Lalo went off island to high school. Maybe she would wither away among all the books with all the words in them until no one could ever find her again unless they opened a book. Or, she might ferment in the library like Mama's back-porch cider that finally exploded.

"So," repeated Lalo, "tomorrow you will buy a plaid dress and the year will begin."

I smiled.

My mother believed in plaid. Plaid meant beginnings. Each year I began school with a plaid dress, then slowly that beginning became the past as I wore jeans and shirts, then shorts when it was hot. In my closet hung five plaid dresses, one for each year, like memorials.

"So," I imitated Lalo, getting up from the rock and grabbing a clump of chickory, "tomorrow, yes, I will buy a plaid dress and your mother will buy you a new lunch box."

"And it will be another year like all the other years," said Lalo happily.

His smile made me smile, but I knew he was wrong. All the years were changed because of what I was missing and no one would talk about. And all the years would be changed even more than Lalo and I knew, for when we walked through the meadow of chickory and meadowsweet, when we climbed up and over the rise to my house, the basket was already in the driveway, a baby sitting in it, crying. My mother stood with her hands up to her face, shocked. My father's face was dark and still and bewildered. Only Byrd looked happily satisfied, as if something wonderful, something wished for, had happened.

And it had.

Her excitement was here.

*Sometimes she dreamed of white hair, like silk, touching her face, and tiny white stones that tumbled. Beach stones, maybe. And crying. She could almost taste the salt of tears when she thought of it; the taste of memory. Why, then, wasn't she frightened when she remembered this?*

# Chapter Three

The baby looked from one face to the other, then suddenly stopped crying. It was quiet then, no one moving, as if we were actors who had forgotten our lines. Lalo moved in front of me, and I looked over his shoulder at Byrd smiling, my father's dark look, my mother tense and pale. Then, we all turned to watch the baby slowly get up to climb out of the basket. Mama's hands went out protectively, fluttering like birds; Byrd took a step, but the baby, legs twisted in a blanket, fell hard on the driveway and began to wail, a sad sound like a lost cat. In one movement Byrd leaned down and swooped the baby up in her arms, and Mama leaned down and picked up a sheet of paper. The paper fluttered in the breeze. Or was it Mama's hand shaking? Lalo reached back and took my hand, pulling me with him as he moved closer. I knew he was protecting me, but from what? The rest was a scene in slow motion, Papa taking the paper out of my mother's hands, reading it to us, my mother beginning to cry. There was no sound to her crying; only tears streaming down her face. I stared at Mama. *I had never seen Mama cry this way. Terrible, somehow, without the sound.*

My father's voice wavered as he read.

"This is Sophie. She is almost a year old and she is good."

*Sophie.* At the sound of her name the baby looked up at him and stopped crying. Papa stared at her for a moment. He swallowed, then continued. Lalo pulled me behind him, and as we came closer Sophie turned to look at us. One of her hands went up to rub her ear.

"I cannot take care of her now, but I know she will be safe with you," Papa read. "I have watched you. You will be a good family. I will lose her forever if you don't do this, so please keep her. I will send money for her when I can. I will come back for her one day. I love her."

Lalo still held my hand. Papa looked at Mama.

"She spelled *please* wrong," he said, his voice soft.

Lalo held out his hand to Sophie in Byrd's arms. Sophie stared, then reached out her hand to touch his. Lalo smiled. A small satisfied sound came from Sophie, and she began to move his hand up and down, staring at him as if waiting for something familiar. Lalo took Sophie's other hand and moved it up and down and suddenly, for the first time, Sophie smiled.

Papa turned to Mama, as if Sophie's smile had given him energy.

"Call the police," he said.

Byrd took a breath, almost a gasp.

"We have to report this," said Papa quickly. "This child has been left. This is a criminal act."

Sophie sucked in her breath, imitating Byrd.

Mama didn't answer. She held out her arms to Sophie, and Sophie looked at her steadily, thoughtfully.

"Sophie?" said Mama softly.

She crooned the name, like a lullaby.

Sophie watched Mama. She put two fingers in her mouth; then, after a moment, she took them out.

"Sophie," she repeated, her voice clear and high like a bell.

She lunged toward Mama then, nearly falling out of Byrd's arms. Mama's arms went around her.

"Lily." Papa's voice was loud. "We need to talk inside. Alone, without the baby."

"Without *Sophie,* John," Mama corrected him.

"Without Sophie," said Papa slowly.

"Sophie," repeated Sophie in her small voice.

Mama smiled and so did Byrd, and they looked at each other as if there were a secret between them, something we didn't know.

"Here," said Mama, handing over Sophie to Byrd. "I'm going inside to speak about criminal acts."

"Oh, boy," whispered Lalo beside me. "Oh, boy."

It was quiet outside, warm and peaceful. No clouds cluttered up the sky. Lalo and I sat in the grass with Sophie, playing patty-cake.

"She knows how," said Lalo with an amazed smile.

"All babies know how," said Byrd. She looked at me. "Someone who loves them always teaches them."

She sat on the steps in her dress and fancy stockings watching Sophie and trying to pretend that there were no sounds of loud voices coming from inside. We could hear Papa's voice, strong and sometimes fierce, then Mama's, that sweet soft way of talking she had when she was serious and angry, like a steady hum.

All of a sudden the voices stopped and the silence made us look up. The door opened. Mama came out first, then Papa. Papa looked tired, the way he looked when he had finished his nightly tap dancing.

Byrd stood up and stared at Mama. Sophie turned and put out one arm toward Mama.

"She will stay with us for a while," said Mama softly.

"Until we can come to some civilized agreement about what to do," said Papa firmly.

Byrd smiled. Papa sat down on the porch steps wearily.

"Oh, boy," said Lalo for the third time.

Byrd lifted Sophie and whirled her around until Sophie laughed. A small island plane flew over our heads and away. And Byrd's pearls broke, showering Sophie and falling over the meadow grasses like tears.

# Chapter Four

It was night, Sophie's first night with us. Moonlight was sliding slowly across my quilt like the tide when I heard her first whimper. There was the scurry of feet, a door opening, then closing, my mother's soft, soothing voice. I turned over and lay looking out the window. Stars were tossed across the sky, a moon nearly full with a small slice off one side. Sophie cried harder, and then a door opened and closed again. I raised my head off the pillow and listened. A new sound came up the stairs. The crying stopped, but I knew the new sound well. I got up and went to the door, opening it. A night-light lighted the hallway. I walked down the cool wood floor, down the stairs, and stopped, my hand on the newel post. One lamp glowed in the living room. Mama sat on the floor holding Sophie. Sophie's face was tear streaked, a sleep line across one cheek. But she stared at my father, her mouth open. His hair was rumpled and his eyes dark circled. He was dressed in pajamas and tap shoes, and he danced on the tiled table. Mama sang along with him.

*Boys and girls together.*
*Me and Mamie O'Rorke*
*Tripped the light fantastic*
*On the sidewalks of New York.*

Papa ended and Mama clapped for him. Sophie still stared at him, her mouth open. Papa got down off the table and Sophie began to clap too.

"Mo," she said. "Mo."

"More," explained Mama.

Papa sighed.

"I know what *mo* means, Lily," he said grumpily.

He looked over and saw me sitting on the lowest step of the stairway.

"I know what *mo* means," he repeated.

He smiled at me suddenly and I smiled back. We were thinking of all the times that Papa danced for me; all the nighttime songs when I was sick, and how hard he had tried to teach me the soft shoe that I couldn't learn.

Sophie yawned, and Mama stood up with her. Sophie laid her head on Mama's shoulder.

"Thank you," Mama whispered to Papa.

She walked past me on the stairway. Sophie's eyes were already closed.

Papa sighed and walked to the screen door, opening it, walking out onto the porch. I followed him.

He sat on the porch steps. I sat next to him.

"Stars," he said to me.

I nodded. I knew that talk of the stars was in place of things we would not say.

"Milky Way," I said. I pointed. "The Pleiades."

Papa put his arm around me.

"Has anyone asked you what *you* think about all of this?"

"Mama doesn't ask those things," I said to him sharply. "Not anymore." The sound of anger in my voice surprised me.

"No," his voice was soft. "But I am asking."

"I never had—" I stopped. "I never had a sister,"

I said slowly. I looked up at Papa and knew that we were both thinking about something else. *Someone* else.

"That's not the question, Lark," said Papa softly.

Insects buzzed in the grass. A gull cried far away over the water.

"I like Sophie," I said. "I don't love her."

"Don't," said Papa. "Don't love her."

He sighed.

"I like her too," he said after a moment.

"Mama will love her soon," I whispered.

"If not already," murmured Papa.

"I'm scared," I said after a while. "For Mama."

There was a silence.

"Yes," said Papa. "But it is not your job to protect her."

I looked up at Papa.

"Is it your job?" I asked.

Papa didn't speak for a moment.

"Not if she won't let me," he said.

We sat for a long time then, watching clouds fall over the moon like nets. After a while I knew there weren't any more words. Not now. I got up and went inside, up the stairs to bed. Soon, just before I fell asleep, I heard the sound downstairs of ice in a glass and then, like messages, my father's dancing. I listened half the night to his taps on the tiles as the moon moved across the sky and away.

❧

"So?" said Lalo at the door. He grinned his crazy morning grin. He probably slept smiling.

My eyes squinted against the hard morning light.

"In the kitchen," I said.

Lalo walked past me. I stood, looking out into the sunlight. Then I slammed the door.

"Good morning to you too," I said, my voice so loud that I surprised myself.

"Hi, Larkin," he called to me over his shoulder before he disappeared into the kitchen.

"So, Sophie!" I heard him say. "It's Lalo!"

I heard Sophie's delighted "La."

I walked into the kitchen and leaned against the counter. Morning sun came in, pouring over Mama's glass bottles in the window. Byrd sat in her velvet bathrobe, the wrinkles on her face like etched glass in the sunlight. Papa drank orange juice as he read the newspaper. Sophie sat in my old high chair, cereal on her face. She grinned at me suddenly.

"La!" she called, holding out her spoon for me.

I couldn't help smiling back at her. Her tiny neat rows of teeth looked like seed pearls in one of Byrd's brooches. And it came to me, then, like the sudden sharp pain in my chest when I swam too fast, that I was not only scared for Mama, I was scared for me. I looked at Papa and he stared back at me. His look was almost like a warning that said, *Don't, Lark. Don't.*

Lalo saw Papa's expression and his smile faded.

I turned and went out of the kitchen and out onto the porch where there was space. I walked down the steps and out onto the lawn, but I could still hear Sophie's high, happy voice. After a moment I went down past the pond and through the fields to the small cemetery that sat on a hill by the water where all I could hear was the sound of the sea and the wind. A tiny stone sat there, surrounded by big headstones with angels and flowers and names engraved on them. There was no name on the tiny stone, just the word BABY and a date that showed that the one buried there had only lived for one day. I felt a movement beside me, and Lalo was there.

"So, Larkin," Lalo began, his voice thin, the words almost blowing away in the wind.

I shook my head. I wanted to talk, but Lalo and I had talked about this many times. It was Mama and Papa I wanted to talk with, but Mama and Papa didn't talk. Not about this.

Beside me Lalo sighed. The wind rippled the unmown grasses. And we stood, silently looking down at the stone that marked the grave of my baby brother.

*Most of all she remembered the man. His hands, strong, brown. She could feel the rumble in his chest when he held her, the sound of song coming up through him and surrounding her, making her smile. Even now she smiled at the thought of it. Sometimes in a crowd of people she would hear a voice, turn, look for him. It was not so much his face she looked for.*

*It was his hands she remembered.*

# Chapter Five

Rock, paper, scissors. Papa tried to teach Sophie the game. They sat on the porch, Sophie in his lap, as Papa held out his hands time after time.

"Rock, paper, see paper, Sophie? Scissors?"

Papa knew she was too young. She couldn't know that paper covered rock, rock crushed scissors, scissors cut paper, but Papa didn't care. Neither did Sophie. There was something about Papa's hands she liked, watching them form rock, paper, scissors. He hid his hands behind his back, and it was not what shape the hands took when they came out of hiding, it was his hands, no matter what, that Sophie liked.

"Mo," said Sophie.

My mother smiled from the porch swing.

"We should teach her words," she said. "Hands, Sophie. Hands."

"Mo," said Sophie, frowning at her.

Papa laughed at the frown and Sophie laughed, too, the sound like water falling over rocks.

"Papa," said my mother. "Say, 'Papa.' "

Slowly, very slowly, Papa stood up. He set Sophie on the porch. He turned to my mother and his quiet anger caused Sophie to stare up at him.

"I'm sorry," said my mother quickly. "I didn't mean that, John."

"Yes, you did, Lily," said Papa. "You meant it. I am not her papa. I am *not*. Somewhere"—his voice faltered and he tried to steady it—"somewhere there is a man who *is* her father. And sometime, maybe soon, her mother will come back for her. She is not yours, Lily. She is *not ours*." He paused and when he spoke again his voice sounded rough, like rock scraping rock. "Sophie is not a substitute," he said slowly.

Mama's mouth opened, then shut. My skin felt like ice suddenly, the way it felt the day of the first spring swim in the bay.

"I'm sorry, Lily," Papa said softly. "It had to be said."

Papa turned and walked down the steps and down the grass to the path that went to town. Sophie held out a hand to him, but his back was turned and he didn't see. My mother stood up and went after him.

Byrd sighed.

"Ah, well. Here we are, alone at last, Sophie," said Byrd, trying to be cheerful.

Byrd turned to Lalo, then to me, her eyes bright with sudden tears.

"This is not meant to be easy," she said. "It is a very important thing to do, for Sophie and especially for your mother and father. But it will not be easy. Do you understand?"

I understood. I did. I knew that what she meant was what Papa had said. Sophie was not ours. Someday she would go away. Another thing to miss.

"Why is it important?" I asked her.

I asked her for me, but mostly for Lalo, who was holding Sophie as if he would never let her go.

"It is important, Larkin, because we are giving Sophie something to take away with her when she goes."

"What?" asked Lalo. "What will she take with her?"

Sophie looked at Lalo and put her fingers up to his lips to feel them move.

"Us," said Byrd firmly.

"And what will we have when she's gone?" I asked.

Byrd looked at me and shook her head because she couldn't speak.

The sun came out suddenly from behind a cloud. Sophie held up her arms to it. And then Lalo asked what none of us had dared to say out loud.

"What if," Lalo said, looking at Sophie, "what if her mother never comes back?"

Byrd studied Lalo for a moment, then looked out to sea as if there was something important out there. She whispered her answer.

"What?" asked Lalo, leaning toward her.

"She will, Lalo," said Byrd. "She *will* come back."

It was late when Mama and Papa came home. Lalo and I had spent the afternoon trying to teach Sophie words. *Good-bye. Larkin. Lalo. Hands.* Byrd and Lalo were setting the table for supper. I sat on the porch,

Sophie sleeping in my arms, when I saw them come up the path from town. They walked slowly up the grass, my father ahead of my mother. Sophie sighed in my lap. I put my arms around her tighter, watching. My mother's face was set, my father's sad.

Sophie woke without crying and sat up, looking at me. Then she turned and saw them. She reached out to my father.

She spoke, the word as clear as an autumn sky.

"Hands," she said.

# Chapter Six

We could not keep Sophie a secret, a small child at our house. We tried inventing stories.

"A niece?" suggested Papa. "A long-lost niece."

"A cousin," said Mama. "A cousin's baby, left for the winter."

"That sounds like hibernation," said Papa.

"Maybe a crown princess," said Byrd with sarcasm, "dropped from a balloon."

So we stopped trying and told the truth. And Sophie became the island's child, loved by everyone, fed by everyone, baby-sat by everyone, read to and carried about and sung to by all.

We took her to Dr. Unfortunato, as Byrd called

him, because of his wife who talked too much. His name was really Dr. Fortunato, and Sophie blew into his stethoscope and made him smile. He read the note from Sophie's mother.

He handed Mama back the note. He looked closely at her.

"How are you with this?" he asked softly.

"Fine," said Mama. "Fine," she said louder.

Dr. Fortunato glanced at Papa quickly, then at Sophie.

"Sophie is healthy," he said. "Has she walked yet?"

"Not by herself," said Mama.

"She climbs the furniture," I said.

"She dances on my feet, holding on," said Papa.

Dr. Fortunato smiled.

"Call me when she does the soft shoe," he said.

Sophie liked carrots and didn't like milk. Beets were for spitting. She hated baths, screaming so hard we had to shut the windows so no one would hear, but she loved to sit in the bay until her skin wrinkled, pouring water from one bucket to another. She napped with Byrd in the afternoons, and Byrd sang every song she knew to Sophie: lullabies, show tunes, hymns, folk songs, and once, in a loud and happy voice, something about a drunken sailor until Papa knocked on the window for her to stop.

School began, and I went off the first day. No plaid dress.

"How come?" I asked Mama.

Mama saw my expression.

"But, Lark, I thought you always hated those plaid dresses," she said.

"I did," I said. "I do."

I smiled at Mama, but my thoughts startled me.

*But I wanted one anyway, Mama.*

Sophie cried when I left. She sat in her pajamas, her arms stretched up to me, her lower lip jutted out.

"La!" she cried mournfully.

"La!" Sophie said, smiling, when Lalo came to walk to school with me.

"I could stay home from school," I said.

"You'll do no such thing," said Mama. "She'll learn that you come back."

At school the library had been freshly painted, the smell of paint mixing with the smell of old books. The shelves were dusted, the books neatly lined up as if daring us to take them down and read them. Ms. Minifred was slicked and clean and ready for us.

"Good morning. Sit up straight, Lalo," she said. "Slumping may stop the blood from going to your brain."

Lalo grinned. Under the library table was his new lunch box, black and shiny like Ms. Minifred's hair. For Lalo another year like all the other years.

"This year we will be talking about the power of language," said Ms. Minifred. "The power of words. And how words can change you."

I stared at Ms. Minifred.

*What about when there are no words?* I thought. *Silence can change you, too, Ms. Minifred.*

Ms. Minifred looked at me, as if she had read my thoughts.

"Words," she said.

She looked away, out the library windows, as if she was hearing words from far away. Then she waved her arm at the library shelves.

"In this room, in these books, there is the power of a hundred hurricanes. Wondrous words," said Ms. Minifred.

Lalo and I looked at each other and smiled. Another year.

Mama was right. Sophie was waiting for us at home, her face pressed against the window, when Lalo and I came up the porch steps at the end of the school day.

The second week of school Sophie took her first step, pushing off from Papa's tiled tap-dancing table. Papa clapped, Byrd smiled, Mama cried, and from then on Sophie walked; sometimes tilted forward as if a wind pushed her; sometimes tottering so that our hands went out to protect her.

Sophie rode the island's dirt roads on a seat on the back of Mama's bicycle, pointing to dogs and cats. She learned to wave by cupping her hand and waving to herself. She learned what the word *hot* meant when she touched the oven door, and that *no* meant *no* when she went near Mama's wet canvases.

And then very suddenly one day she began to put her hands behind her back and bring them out in fists, hands flat, or two-fingered shapes.

"Rock, paper, scissors," said Papa softly. "Sophie learned. She doesn't know what it means, but she learned."

Mama smiled.

"That's how it is with children," said Byrd. She paused. "Someday, she will remember all of this in some way, you know."

We looked at Byrd, then at Sophie. Mama turned from the window, her smile fading, all of us thinking of Sophie's mother. Papa watched Mama. It was as if Byrd, in one sentence, had pulled Sophie back from us to a place where we couldn't follow.

Sophie got up unsteadily and looked at Papa. She picked up one foot and put it down. She did it again.

"The shuffle," whispered Mama. "She wants you to dance."

Mama watched Papa.

"She wants you to dance," she repeated, her voice so thin, it almost broke.

There was a silence. Then Papa leaned over and picked up Sophie. Slowly he began to dance holding her, Sophie beginning to grin at him. But Papa didn't grin back at her. He looked at Mama as he sang.

*Me and my shadow*
*Strolling down the avenue.*
*Me and my shadow,*

*Not a soul to tell our troubles to.*
*And when it's twelve o'clock,*
*We climb the stair;*
*We never knock*
*For nobody's there.*


Papa and Sophie danced a long time, the late afternoon light falling over them like a spotlight. Mama watched, standing by the window. Byrd sat, straight as a tree. Only Lalo smiled.

"Come, Larkin," called Papa. "Dance with us."

I shook my head. "I can't," I said.

The next day Sophie's letter came, almost as if Byrd's words about Sophie's mother had made it happen. Five one-dollar bills slipped out of the letter in Mama's hand as she read.

*Dear Sophie,*
    *Happy birthday. I love you. I think of you every hour, every minute of every day.*
    *Don't forget me.*

                        *Love,*
                        *Mama*

# Winter

*She loved the wind and she loved music. She remembered them together; the sound of the wind in the marsh grass and a song that she dreamed, a thread sound of song that she couldn't remember when she woke.*

# Chapter Seven

Winter came fast with a surprising sudden snow
the day before Thanksgiving. We bought Sophie
a snowsuit, red boots, and mittens, knowing that
the snow would never last. Island snow never lasted.
Sophie didn't like the mittens; she didn't like the
snowsuit; she didn't like snow. Sophie did like her
red rubber boots, shuffling around the house in
them during the day, taking them to bed with her
that night.

We ate Thanksgiving dinner in the dining room;
the glasses gleaming, candles lighted, Sophie in her
red boots. Dr. Fortunato stopped by on his way to
see Rollie's wife, who had a temperature, but he

really came to see Sophie. Griffey came to eat with us, and he played his accordion for Sophie. She liked "Roll Out the Barrel" and loved "Amazing Grace."

"Mo," said Sophie. "Mo."

"You'd better learn some new songs," said Byrd.

"I'm working on it," said Griffey, insulted. "The sewer business is busy, you know."

Griffey began to play "Amazing Grace" again.

"She loves this song," he said to Byrd. "She does."

Byrd nodded.

"She has taste, this child," said Byrd.

Later we walked to town, everyone coming out to say hello and to wave to Sophie and to call happy Thanksgiving from their porches. The light sat like porcelain on the water; the sea calm, the sky the gray of silver-dollar plants.

That night Papa danced good-night for Sophie, dancing "Me and My Shadow" over and over. Lalo taught Sophie how to blow a kiss. Mama got out her sketchbook and began to draw Sophie, the lamp spilling light over her work. I looked over her shoulder as she drew Sophie, all rounded edges, and then the sharper larger figure of Papa holding her.

"Do you think she remembers?" I asked her suddenly.

Mama looked up at me. Her eyes shone bright.

"Remembers?"

"Remembers her mother," I said. "Do you think she misses her?"

Mama stared at me.

"I don't know," she said after a moment. "But it doesn't matter, Larkin. We're doing the right thing." Mama sat back and looked at me. "You know that, don't you? Sometimes you have to do what is right."

*What is right.* I didn't answer, but I felt my face grow hot with sudden anger. There were words in the spaces between us; those words we had never spoken, words about what *I* thought was right. It was hard to say what I thought without getting rid of those words first. Mama, staring at me as if she knew my thoughts, suddenly straightened her shoulders and went back to her drawing. Conversation was over, that one subject that stood between us closed. I watched her sketch, hating the look of her hand slipping across the paper as if she was brushing away all the words I needed to hear. Papa and Sophie came to life on the page, the two of them sitting in a chair by the fireplace now; Sophie imitating Papa—*rock, paper, scissors*—her hands, almost like Mama's: quick shadows like butterflies in the firelight.

"They never named him," I said.

We stood on Lalo's favorite place on the island, the north cliffs that stood high above the water. Lalo liked the high places, the dangerous edges of the island that always scared me. *He isn't afraid of anything*. Lalo looked at me for a moment. His hair blew across his face. He turned, then threw a rock out over the water. He leaned down to watch the rock disappear, a tiny splash from where we stood. I shivered and pulled my hat down over my ears, hooking my fingers in Lalo's belt as I always did.

Lalo straightened and smiled at me. This was his favorite cold, windy weather, too, and he only wore a sweatshirt.

"I won't fall, Larkin. I never fall, so stop worrying. Remember? Once I slept in a tree."

I remembered. His mother had once taken him to a new barber who cut Lalo's hair too short. Lalo hid from everyone, spending a day and a night up the tree by the pond until his mother lured him down with kale soup and cake.

"You haven't fallen yet," I said. I looked out at the water, gray and dark, whitecaps everywhere. "But things happen when you don't think they will. Things happen that you've never even thought about. Ever."

We began to walk the cliff path toward town.

"So," said Lalo. I could see his breath hang in a cloud. "It's only been six months since he"—Lalo looked sideways at me before he finished—"since he died. Mama said it takes people time. She says it's different for different people."

I didn't say anything. Lalo picked up another rock and drew back his arm to throw it.

"Why didn't they name him?" I asked.

Lalo paused, then threw the rock way out over the water.

"So," he said, his hair lifting strangely in the wind, "*you* name him."

I stopped.

"What?"

"You always do that," said Lalo. "You always say, 'What?' when you don't know what to say. Or you don't want to answer. The fact is, if you need him named, then you name him."

I stared at Lalo and he stared back. Then he

turned and began walking again. I stood, watching him as he walked down through the beach plum; past the clumps of chickory gone by; past the juniper bushes.

"You're dumb," I yelled at Lalo. "You're so dumb. The very dumbest!"

The sky darkened above suddenly, a cloud in front of the sun, like in a movie when it was suddenly serious and you'd better pay attention. Lalo disappeared over the hill and I stopped yelling. Then, after a moment, he appeared, looking at me.

I looked at the sea again, then I walked after him. When I reached him he was sitting by the old scrub oak tree that perched at the edge of the cliff.

I stood next to him and looked down on the town. I could see a car moving along Main Street, the church spire in the middle, a fishing boat coming into the harbor.

"It wouldn't matter, you know," I said. "It wouldn't matter as much, except—" I stopped.

Lalo looked up at me.

"Except that Sophie's here," he said.

Tears came then, I couldn't stop them, flooding down my face, cold and startling. Lalo didn't move. He didn't come over to put his arm around me, or put his hand on my arm. He just stared out over the water. And I cried, thinking about what my father had said to me not so long ago.

"Don't love her," he had said to me about Sophie.

*Don't worry, Papa. I don't know how to love Sophie. I don't know how to love Sophie because I don't know how to love my brother.*

I cried.

Lalo sat under the tree, not looking at me.

The sun came out.

# Chapter Eight

"My Wish for the World."

Portia Pinter stood in front of the class, reading in her high voice.

Someone snorted.

Ms. Minifred gave a piercing look to the back, probably to Ozzie, who always snorted. He had four brothers who snorted too. Lalo said it was part of the family tradition.

"My Wish for the World," repeated Portia, pushing up her glasses, "is for world peace and homes for stray animals, especially cats."

Another snort. Ms. Minifred smiled.

Portia, short with jeweled eyeglasses, had told us

once she had relatives in the royal family of England. Lalo called her Princess Portia.

Portia's voice droned on. We were in the library, where water was leaking down the walls. It had rained for three days straight, so hard and fierce that at home Mama put towels on the windowsills and under the door where the water streamed in. Papa left early for work and came home in the evening wearing his yellow slicker, the wind nearly blowing him down the hill. Byrd sang songs and read books to Sophie, who happily pointed out new streams of water.

At school we had all helped move the books to the middle of the room, and Rebel, the janitor, had come up from the basement to turn off the electricity. Rebel had come to the island with his Harley-Davidson motorcycle when he was eighteen and had never left. That was fifteen years ago. We had seen pictures of him then, and he hadn't changed. He was still thin, and his hair stood straight up. He had a mysterious tattoo on his arm that said "Wild Eunice."

Rebel liked Ms. Minifred. Rebel and Ms. Minifred read books together. Lalo and I had come late to the school library one afternoon, and they had been at a library table, Rebel sitting on a child's chair, smiling, his chin resting on his knees as he read to Ms. Minifred.

Rebel had a bookcase in the basement filled with books. Lalo had seen it once when he went down to borrow a screwdriver.

"All poetry," Lalo had said, impressed.

"That's because Rebel is anguished," said Portia. "All anguished people read poetry. He has a lost love somewhere. Eunice, you know. Ms. Minifred is helping him through the power of wondrous words."

Ozzie snorted.

"He has lots of loves," he scoffed. "I've seen him around town with girls on the back of his Harley."

"They are only temporary," said Portia, her jeweled glasses gleaming in the darkened room, "until Wild Eunice returns."

Today Rebel stood at the back, listening to Portia, his tool chest at his feet, his arms folded so we could see Wild Eunice on his arm; red letters with green ivy surrounding them in a violent sort of way. He had never stayed in class before. He had always come to work, then disappeared back into his room in the basement. I thought suddenly of the day that Griffey's goat had jumped his fence and walked through town and into the school, a strange sight in the schoolroom, interrupting the familiar rhythm of the class. Somehow Rebel seemed too big for the room, filling it up with leather and spiked hair.

Rebel saw me watching him, and he mouthed the words *How's Sophie?*

*Fine,* I mouthed back. *Walking.*

Rebel smiled broadly.

"Also," Portia went on, "it would be quite excellent to have clean air, clean water, and clean houses. In conclusion," said Portia, stopping to take a breath, "cleanliness is next to godliness."

Portia looked at the class. "My mother says so," she added.

A snort from the back.

"Thank you, Portia," said Ms. Minifred.

"There's redundancy there," said Rebel.

Everyone turned to look at Rebel, who never spoke up when he was in the room.

"Yes, most assuredly there is," said Ms. Minifred. "You don't need to say 'quite excellent,' Portia. *Excellent* is its own definition. It stands alone."

"Yep," said Rebel, picking up his toolbox and

pausing at the door to look at Ms. Minifred. "It doesn't get any better than excellent."

There was what Ms. Minifred called a "pulsing silence" as Rebel went out the door. Then Ms. Minifred spoke.

"Yep, indeed," said Ms. Minifred, her face flushed. "Wondrous words spoken by Rebel. It doesn't get any better than excellent."

Lalo and I looked at each other. It was, of course, the *yep* that did it. In that moment, the room so damp that my hair had begun to curl on its own, Lalo and I knew that there was more than words between Rebel and Ms. Minifred.

Lalo leaned over to whisper.

"So. Do you think anyone else noticed?"

I shook my head. Everyone else was rustling papers.

"Poor Ms. Minifred if Wild Eunice ever finds out," I whispered back.

Lalo grinned suddenly at me, then at Ms. Minifred.

"I think Ms. Minifred can take care of herself," he said softly.

And then, Ms. Minifred looked up suddenly and smiled at us. A real smile, with teeth.

"Tomorrow is poetry," she said. Her smile grew

wider. "All the world can be found in poetry. All you need to see and hear. All the moments, good and bad, joyous and sad."

Lalo leaned close to me.

"Rebel will be back," he whispered.

*All the world.*

Lalo and I walked home through town, the wind pushing us along, our feet wet even though we wore rubber boots. The harbor was black, waves topped with gray. We passed the newspaper building, and I looked in and saw Papa reading at his desk, his reading lamp shining on the wood. We passed the hardware store and the drugstore and FOOD MART with the D missing so it read FOO MART.

I pulled my slicker around me and held my rain hat on to keep it from blowing away.

*All you need to see and hear.*

Lalo tugged at my arm.

"What?"

"Home," said Lalo.

I looked up and saw the inn, the porch all wet and windswept. Lalo pulled me up the steps, and we took off our hats, standing there, listening to the rain on the porch roof.

"So?" Lalo said.

"I'm thinking about poetry," I said.

"I knew that," said Lalo matter-of-factly.

"And what Ms. Minifred said."

Lalo nodded.

"And I'm thinking about—" I began.

"The world," said Lalo.

I looked at Lalo.

"Poetry is just words," I said.

"That's all we've got," said Lalo.

I stared at Lalo. The rain came harder.

And when I left Lalo and ran up through the wind and rain to my house and opened the door, Mama and Sophie were at the kitchen table, Sophie covered with finger paint, her fingers squishing the red on the white paper. My mother turned, and on her face were tiny finger marks where Sophie had touched her. They had dried there as if she had left her marks on Mama forever. They both smiled at me, and Sophie reached out her hands to touch me too.

*Ms. Minifred's wrong,* I thought, as I left my slicker dripping in the hallway and went to join them. *There are no words for this.*

*She remembered the color red: red flowers that bloomed in winter, cold red sunsets, and especially a tiny teardrop of red that glowed like fire in the light. She now wore it around her neck, but when she thought of it she could remember the feel of it in her hand, how her fingers curled around it. Sometimes she opened her hand, expecting to see it there shining in the pocket of her palm.*

*Red had always made her happy.*

# Chapter Nine

In the night I woke to hear the rain turn to ice, the sound like rocks against the roof and windows. When I slept again I dreamed. I was cold in my dream, so cold that goose bumps rose on my arms, and when I breathed out my breath hung in a cloud of ice. In my dream the fields were ice covered, the sea was frozen, the waves spiking in gleaming glass waves. Far off Sophie was walking away from the island in her red boots.

"Baby!" I called to her, but she didn't turn around. She walked across the harbor, around the fishing boats frozen in place.

"Come back, Baby!" I screamed.

In my dream Byrd came to stand next to me.

"Call her by her name," Byrd said sadly. "Call her Sophie."

Tears sat frozen on her cheeks like diamonds. I stared at her, but when I turned back it was too late. Sophie had walked past the breakwater and was gone.

"La."

Fingers poked at my eyes.

"La."

I woke in the darkened room, the dream slipping away. Sophie sat on my bed in her blue woolly pajamas with the feet. Her red boots were next to my pillow.

"La."

Sophie's cold fingers touched the tears on my cheeks.

I sat up in bed. The air was cold in my bedroom, though early light shone in along the edges of the window shades. I leaned over and pulled up the shade. Ice sat thick on the inside of the windows. Outside there was ice everywhere, the telephone lines and the roads covered, the trees bending over with the weight. The fields were still and shining, like my dream.

I pulled Sophie under the covers with me, tucking them around us.

"Sophie!" Mama called down the hallway.

"Sophie!" called Sophie, imitating her.

"There you are," said Mama in the doorway. "The electricity is off, Larkin. Papa's making a fire. You'd better stay in bed until we get some heat in the living room."

Mama came over close to the bed and looked down at us. Behind her Byrd appeared, dressed in her velvet robe, heavy socks, earrings, and a hat. I smiled.

"Don't mention how I look," warned Byrd.

"Brrr," said Sophie, reaching out a hand to her.

"She said Byrd!" said Mama, smiling at Byrd. "Sophie's beginning to say more than her name. At last!"

"Lily! The fire's ready." Papa's voice came from downstairs.

Mama turned and went down the hallway, pulling her sweater around her.

Byrd sat on my bed and took Sophie's hand.

"Hand," said Sophie.

"No school," Byrd said to me.

I sighed.

"No poetry," I said.

After a moment I looked at Byrd.

"What do you know about poetry?" I asked Byrd.

Byrd smiled and shivered. I opened the covers for her and she got in, Sophie between us. Sophie reached over and played with the ruby that hung on the gold chain around Byrd's neck.

"Poetry is a way of taking life by the throat," said Byrd. "That's what Robert Frost said."

"Ms. Minifred says that poetry shows us the world," I said.

Byrd smiled.

"Words are uppermost in Ms. Minifred's life," she said.

"Do you think words have answers?" I asked.

Byrd took off her necklace and handed it to Sophie.

"La," said Sophie happily.

She looked at it closely, turning it over and over in her hand.

"Do you?" I asked Byrd. "Think words have answers?"

"It depends on your questions," said Byrd. "But"—she turned her head to look at me over

Sophie—"you should know that there are some things for which there are no answers, no matter how beautiful the words may be."

I stared at her.

"Sometimes poetry—words—give us a small, lovely look at ourselves," said Byrd. "And sometimes that is enough."

There was silence.

"Sometimes," Byrd added in a soft voice.

"I had a dream," I said. "You were in it."

"A good dream?"

"No," I said. "Sophie walked away across the icy sea and never once looked back at us."

Byrd was quiet, and we watched Sophie open and close her small hand around the ruby. After a moment Byrd sighed.

"That's the way it will be, Larkin," she said.

"In the dream I called Sophie Baby. You told me to call her by her name," I said.

"Baby," said Sophie, putting her hand on my lips.

"Baby," I said, smiling at her.

We lay in silence, the three of us, as the sun rose and came in through the window and over us. Outside the island glistened.

"Why didn't Mama and Papa name the baby?" I asked.

Byrd didn't look surprised.

"Have you asked them?"

I shook my head.

"No," said Byrd. "For now it is too new, too close to them to talk about. They are busy trying to protect each other."

She turned and looked at me.

"You are wondering right now who is protecting *you*, aren't you?" she asked.

I didn't answer. Sophie came out from under the covers.

"I never saw the baby, Byrd," I whispered. "Not once. And he doesn't have a name."

"I know." Byrd whispered too. "But that is for your mama and papa to do. You will have to find your way. Your dream is like a poem, you know. It put in words what you think about but can't say. Maybe that's what poems do. Maybe this is what Ms. Minifred knows."

I looked out the window for a moment, then I turned back to Byrd.

"Byrd?"

"Yes, dear."

"Words are not uppermost in Ms. Minifred's life anymore."

"Is that so?"

"Ms. Minifred and Rebel are in love. She said 'yep' yesterday. Just like Rebel."

At this Byrd raised her head off the pillow.

"She said 'yep'?"

"Yep," I said.

Byrd began to laugh, and I laughed too. Sophie peered at us, sitting back on her heels, smiling.

"Baby," I said. "Hello, Baby."

The smells of coffee and toast cooking in the fireplace came up from downstairs. And Byrd and I lay in bed with the sun coming in across the quilt, watching Sophie open and close her hand over the ruby.

Open, close. Open, close. Open, close.

# Chapter Ten

Six days of ice.

Six days of no electricity.

No school because of water leaks.

And then, suddenly, without any warning, Sophie began to speak in sentences.

We'd spent hours in front of the fireplace. We'd eaten toast cooked over the fire and soup from the soup pot, when Sophie stood up and looked at us and said, "Food not good."

Lalo loved it. He had come over to our house, wrapped like a mummy. He wore a wool hat, wool gloves, wool-lined boots, and a great wool scarf that Byrd said could have covered his mother's grand piano. Mama laughed when she opened the door.

"Lalo? Are you in disguise?"

"My mother," explained Lalo as he came in quickly. "She thinks germs cannot penetrate wool. Her words."

Papa and Mama smiled. Lalo's mother, Marvella, was efficient, running a forty-two-room inn. She was also beautiful and tall with long black hair, and she had come to the island fifteen years ago and fallen in love right off with Lalo's father, who was then a fisherman. She had convinced him to buy the inn.

"I don't want you to fish. I'm scared of water. It makes me sick," she had said.

"But this is an island, surrounded by water," he'd told her.

I thought Marvella was perfect, and brave to be living in a place that scared her because she loved Lalo's father. Even her name was perfect, Marvella Baldelli. She cooked dishes with wonderful names, too, like *Provençale* and *scallopini* and *francese*. She did, however, have "flawed ideas"—Lalo's words— about electricity.

"Don't stand near the sockets, sweet girl," she told me when I visited, pulling me to the center of the room as if the electricity lurked in the sockets, waiting to hurl its arc forward. She always called me "sweet girl."

Lalo dropped his wool in the hallway and went looking for Sophie.

"How's your mother?" asked Mama, following him into the living room.

"At peace. There's no electricity," said Lalo.

Papa laughed.

Lalo saw Sophie. He smiled.

"So hello, Sophie."

"So, Lalo," said Sophie in a friendly, precise manner. "I want hot cereal."

"So how did that happen?" Lalo asked Mama, amazed.

Mama shook her head.

"Children speak at different times, in different ways," she said. "Larkin spoke early but never said her *d*'s."

"She called me 'Gaggy' instead of 'Daddy,'" said Papa.

"You hated it," said Mama, smiling at him. "You were insulted."

"Just think," said Lalo, "she has all these words

inside her, all the things she's heard us say. She has *sentences* in her, sitting there, waiting to come out."

"Like your mother's electricity," I said, making Papa smile.

We all looked at Sophie, as if she were a book about to be opened. Or written, maybe.

"So we could teach her all sorts of things," said Lalo. He paused and looked at me. "Like poetry."

I frowned.

"Words. Just words," I said.

"Poetry?" Papa said softly. "Just words?" He looked at Mama.

"How do I love thee, let me count the ways . . ."

Mama looked up quickly. She smiled suddenly, a new look to her. Or an old look that I remembered.

"The fog comes in on little cat feet," said Byrd to Sophie.

"Cat feet," said Sophie. She pronounced the words carefully, like Ms. Minifred talking to Ozzie. We laughed. Sophie liked the sound of it, both the words and the laughter.

"Cat feet," she repeated.

We laughed again, and Papa put his arm around Mama. Sophie pulled at Papa's other hand. Mama and Papa got up, Mama lifting Sophie up too,

Byrd's ruby around her neck gleaming on her blue pajamas. They danced together, the three of them. Sophie's arms went around them both as Lalo and Byrd and I watched, her small fat hands resting on their necks.

Lalo was quiet, watching.

They danced in the cold room to no music, though it seemed that music played.

"I like this," said Lalo.

Byrd smiled.

I liked it, too, Mama's face soft and smiling the way it used to be, Papa's arms around her. I wanted it to last forever, Mama and Papa dancing in slow circles, Sophie making them smile again.

Lalo moved closer to Byrd and me.

"Maybe Sophie will stay," he said after a moment, his voice soft.

I couldn't speak. Byrd reached over and took my hand.

Sophie cupped her hand and waved to me. I waved back, and there was a sudden sharp pain in my throat as I thought about Papa's warning not to love Sophie. *It's too late, Papa. Too late.* I looked quickly at Byrd and saw her face, her eyes dark and bright at the same time. It was too late for all of us.

The lights flickered then, and went on, and I held my breath, afraid that the dance would end. But only Sophie saw. She pointed to the lamp in the corner and, as if she, too, didn't want the moment to end, she whispered to us.

"There is light."

*She remembered voices. And words like whispers in her ear. Words like the soft wind, touching her.*

*Words.*

# Chapter Eleven

The ice melted, the roads were cleared, and everything went back to the way it was. It was as if Mama and Papa hadn't put their arms around each other, as if Papa hadn't said words of poetry to her, as if Mama hadn't been happy for that little while.

Papa went back to his silences and his work and his nighttime tap-dancing on the tiles for Sophie. Mama went back to her studio, painting for the afternoon hours when Sophie napped. I didn't know what she was painting. There was no paint on her at the end of the day, no signs of what took her time, only a half smile when Papa asked her how it was going.

"Better," she said with a tilt of her head. "Hard, but better."

Byrd went back to her room behind the pocket doors, leaving them open wide enough for Sophie to walk in and out, and me, of course. Sophie dressed up in Byrd's velvet hat with the diamond clip, and the wide-brimmed straw with the long red ribbon, and lace and beads. And always the red ruby. They read books, Sophie talking and turning the pages and pointing. Byrd's voice was smooth, like the velvet of her hat.

*"so much depends*
*upon*

*a red wheel*
*barrow*

*glazed with rain*
*water*

*beside the white*
*chickens."*

"That's William Carlos Williams," Byrd said to Sophie.

"She doesn't understand," I said.

"She doesn't need to understand, dear," said Byrd. "She likes the way the words sound."

Sophie sat on the bed, Byrd's jet beads around her neck, the black velvet hat on her head. She looked at Byrd and pointed to the page.

"Read," she said. "Please."

Byrd smiled at me.

"She's not a baby anymore, you know. She's growing up."

"Not baby," said Sophie.

There was a small sound behind me and I turned. Mama was in the doorway watching.

"Not baby," Sophie said to Mama.

Mama looked at Sophie for a moment, as if studying her. Then she turned and was gone.

Sophie opened her hand and showed Byrd the ruby lying there.

Byrd looked at me. She sighed.

"Sophie should have that ruby," she said. "Don't you think, Larkin? Someday when I'm not here."

*Someday*. I swallowed.

"Larkin?"

"Yes," I said. "Yes."

"That's good," said Byrd, settling back with her

book. She had a satisfied look, as if something had been settled. But it wasn't settled for me. I didn't want to think about someday. Someday Sophie might go away. Someday Byrd might not be here.

I watched Sophie lean back against Byrd and listen to Byrd read poetry.

Sophie looked up at me as Byrd read.

*"Who has seen the wind?*
*Neither you nor I;*
*But when the trees bow down their heads*
*The wind is passing by."*

"Wind," whispered Sophie. She held out her hands and did rock, paper, scissors.

Byrd smiled as she read and held out her hand and did the same, her wrinkled hand with the long fingers and the wide rose-gold wedding ring. Rock, paper, scissors.

When we went back to school Rebel had fixed the roof, Portia had new shining braces on her teeth, and Ms. Minifred wore red lipstick and large hanging gold earrings in the shape of half moons.

We went to the library for the last period of the day, and Lalo's mouth hung open when he saw Ms. Minifred.

"I thought she was *old*," he whispered. "What happened?"

"Love happened," I said. "She is old. She just doesn't *look* old."

"No," said Lalo. "She looks wondrous."

She did look wondrous.

"Get ready for wondrous words," I said.

"Good afternoon. Sit up, Lalo. Remember the blood flow. Today poetry," said Ms. Minifred, smiling.

Words. Only words.

"I'm not going to lecture you about what poetry is, or how it's written," said Ms. Minifred. "Or even why it's written. You can look that up in books. Instead, I'm going to tell you a story about me."

Portia turned and smiled at Lalo and me; her braces and her glasses glittered. Ozzie didn't snort. He sat up, interested.

"And when my story is finished, class is over," said Ms. Minifred.

Rebel appeared from the hallway and leaned against the wall behind Ms. Minifred, his arms folded.

"When I was a girl, when I was twelve, my older brother William died," said Ms. Minifred. "I loved him. He was good to me. He read me stories and poetry. He wanted to be a writer, and he once said to me that words were comforting. Words had power, he told me. There was no way I could accept his death."

Ms. Minifred paused, and I felt a chill across my arms. No one moved. No one spoke. No one whispered. Rebel kept his eyes on Ms. Minifred.

"There was a funeral. There were flowers. Many people came, and many words were spoken. But their words didn't help. Their words had no power. I was angry," said Ms. Minifred. "I was angry with my brother for leaving me." Ms. Minifred looked down at her hands. "I am still angry," she said softly. "And then I found a poem among my brother's books. He had marked this poem, so I knew it was important to him. When I read it I felt a strange and powerful comfort—not because it made me feel better, but because it said what I felt."

Ms. Minifred opened a book, an old book with worn pages.

"The poem is by Edna St. Vincent Millay. You may not understand it. That's all right. *I* understand it. And William understood it."

No one coughed or sneezed. Everyone was still. I thought of Byrd saying Sophie didn't have to understand the words.

"It is called 'Dirge Without Music.' "

Ms. Minifred began to read.

*"I am not resigned to the shutting away of loving*
*hearts in the hard ground.*
*So it is and so it will be, for so it has been, time out of*
*mind:*
*Into the darkness they go, the wise and the lovely.*
*Crowned*
*With lilies and with laurel they go; but I am not*
*resigned.*

*Lovers and thinkers, into the earth with you.*
*Be one with the dull, the indiscriminate dust.*
*A fragment of what you felt, of what you knew,*
*A formula, a phrase remains,—but the best is lost.*

*The answers quick and keen, the honest look, the*
*laughter, the love,—*
*They are gone. They are gone to feed the roses. Elegant*
*and curled*
*Is the blossom. Fragrant is the blossom. I know. But I*
*do not approve.*

*More precious was the light in your eyes than all the*
*roses in the world.*

*Down, down, down into the darkness of the grave*
*Gently they go, the beautiful, the tender, the kind;*
*Quietly they go, the intelligent, the witty, the brave.*
*I know. But I do not approve. And I am not*
*resigned."*

There was a terrible silence in the room. Ms. Minifred put down the book very carefully. She looked at us, but didn't say anything. We sat still, staring at her.

After a moment Rebel stepped forward, standing in front of Ms. Minifred the way Lalo stood in front of me sometimes.

"Class is over," Rebel said quietly. "Go home."

# Chapter Twelve

I shut the front door softly, leaning against it, hardly breathing. Byrd's door was open, and when I walked past I saw her asleep, Sophie curled beside her. Lalo's voice echoed in my head. He had called to me as I got up from that library room and walked past Ms. Minifred and Rebel and out the door. He had called my name as I walked away from the school and then started to run toward home.

The house was quiet, and I knew Mama was in her studio. I went to Papa's book-lined study, shutting the door behind me. I found the book right away, *Collected Poems,* Edna St. Vincent Millay. It had been read, I could tell. The pages had been turned and looked at and read, and I was angry suddenly, and frightened by it. The anger came up from my stomach and sat in my throat like a shout about to be let go. How could he have read this and not told me? All the months of *silence*. All the times we talked about stars and planets and Sophie. How could he?

I sat in the big chair by his desk and found the poem.

*I am not resigned to the shutting away of loving*
     *hearts in the hard ground.*

I put my hand over the page, hiding the words. All the way home I had thought that it was the library: that it was Ms. Minifred looking so wonderful and sad as she read, and most of all, Rebel coming forward to protect Ms. Minifred. But it wasn't. It wasn't just those things. It was the poem.

*Into the darkness they go, the wise and the lovely.*

I put the book facedown on the desk. Then, very slowly, I picked it up again and went out the door and to Mama's studio. I didn't knock. I opened the door and walked in and saw Mama, and as if I dreamed it, she slowly turned from a painting, her mouth opening to ask me what was the matter, her eyes so blue in the north light of the room.

"Larkin! What's wrong?"

I gave her the book, opened to the poem, and the anger finally came out of me.

"I never saw the baby!" I said softly. "And you never named him!" I began to cry. My voice rose. "And you never talked to me about him!"

The tears came down my face and Mama took me in her arms, the book falling to the floor.

"Larkin, Larkin," she said over and over. "I didn't know."

"You should have known," I said, my voice muffled in her shoulder. "You're my mother."

Mama didn't say anything for a moment.

"I haven't been a good mother to you," she said softly.

I leaned back and looked at her.

"No, but you've been a good mother to Sophie," I said.

And then Mama began to cry, and she scared me. It was as if she hadn't cried ever before and needed to make up all that time without tears. The tears came down her face and over my hair. We stood that way for a long time. And then Mama stopped and stepped back, wiping her eyes with the back of her hand. And I saw her easel behind her. There was a painting there, not finished, all bathed in white. There was light all around a small face with a tiny mouth, and the clear, dark eyes of a baby.

I stared at it for a long time.

"That's the way he was," she said.

I nodded. I stared at the painting for a long time. Then I looked up at Mama.

"Can we name him William?" I asked.

Mama didn't answer.

# Chapter Thirteen

Sophie and I sat by the windows in Lalo's parents' big kitchen, Sophie patting the poinsettia plant on the table.

"That is red," I told her.

"That is red," she repeated.

Lalo's father was setting up the Christmas tree in the lobby, and from behind the closed kitchen door we could hear his father cursing loudly. Lalo grinned.

"Merry Christmas," he said.

Interested, Sophie looked up and pointed to the door as Marvella came rushing through, leaning on it as if to shut out his words.

"She didn't hear that, did she?" she asked,

breathless. "He always curses when he puts up the Christmas tree."

"That's *our* family tradition," Lalo said to me.

"Man is not glad," said Sophie with a frown.

"Oh, dear," Marvella moaned. "Are you hungry, Sophie?"

Marvella hoped that food would interest Sophie. More loud words came from behind the door.

"Toast!" said Marvella loudly. "How about toast, sweet girls?"

Lalo got up and put a slice of bread in the toaster.

"Put slices in both sides remember, Lalo," said Marvella.

Lalo smirked at me.

"My mother thinks that if you don't fill up both sides of the toaster, electricity will leak out the empty side."

"Leakage," said Marvella, nodding.

The door opened and Lalo's father and Papa came in. Sophie looked up and smiled.

"Dammit," she said.

Papa and I walked home together, Sophie between us holding on to Papa's hand and mine. She wore her jacket and red boots, and we swung her up over puddles and curbs. The sun was behind a cloud, and the light slanted across the water and over the boats so that they looked like they'd been washed in silver. Herring gulls flew above us, and ringbills, too, with their fast, easy wing beats. Far off, the ferry came into sight. Sophie switched hands, walking backwards between us.

"You're silly, Sophie," said Papa, smiling at her.

"Silly Sophie," said Sophie.

Papa laughed.

"Silly Sophie," said Papa. "That's almost a poem."

"Yes," I said.

"Words," said Papa, softly. "Did you know that words have a life? They travel out into the air with the speed of sound, a small life of their own, before they disappear. Like the circles that a rock makes when it's tossed into the middle of the pond."

I smiled at the thought of it.

"You used to frown at words," said Papa.

"Until Ms. Minifred," I said.

"She walks in beauty, Ms. Minifred does," said Papa. "That's a poem."

"I know," I said. "I found it in your books."

Papa looked at me for a moment. We lifted

Sophie high over a dog that lay sleeping on the sidewalk.

"I used to say that poem to your mother before she married me," said Papa. "I used to write her poems, and call her up to read poetry to her. Once, I stood under her window and shouted a Shakespeare sonnet to her until she threw a glass of water down on me."

I could feel my heart beating. Everything seemed still, even Sophie between us, the only sound the lonely cries of the gulls. I thought of Papa when he was young, trying to get Mama to love him with words.

"It would be good," I said, "if you still did that."

Papa looked quickly at me. Then he sighed, a sound that made Sophie look up at him.

"You grew up, Larkin," said Papa so softly that I almost missed his words. "You grew up almost without me noticing."

Papa looked straight ahead, his face sad.

"And it wasn't behind my back, Lark." He sighed again. "It was right in front of me. And still I hardly saw it," he whispered.

I could feel tears in the corners of my eyes. "You were busy," I whispered, my throat tight.

Sophie looked at Papa, then at me.

"Busy," she whispered.

Papa stopped walking and dropped Sophie's hand. He gathered me up in his arms.

It had been a long time since he had held me like this, and I held on. I wound my legs around him and laid my head against his neck, and his smell that I remembered from when I was little finally made the tears come. Above, the birds cried, and Sophie reached over and took hold of my foot. But she didn't speak.

Papa kept me in his arms, holding me tighter, until the whistle of the ferry sounded when it passed the breakwater. Then, he bent down and picked up Sophie, holding the two of us. Sophie smiled and smiled at us, and the ferry came into the harbor.

"I love you, Lark," said Papa. "I love you."

"Love," said Sophie, touching Papa's mouth.

I thought about that word, *love,* with Papa's arms around me. That word with a life of its own, traveling out over the town, over the water, out into the world, flying above all of us like the birds.

Love.

# Spring

*There were clouds in all her dreams. She liked their names: cirrus, cumulus, and another one just out of reach of her memory. She didn't remember ever learning the names of clouds.*

*Sometimes she thought she was born knowing them.*

# Chapter Fourteen

"There are three things to remember about spring on the island," old man Brick said. "One, it comes after winter. Two, it comes after winter. Three, it comes after winter and you think it's still winter."

Island winters were always long, flurries of snow when what we had longed for were drifts of it, rain when we wanted sun. Spring came after without change, except for more rain that made us cold.

"Cold to the bone," said Byrd.

She got out the black lace long underwear she'd decorated with jewels and wore it from October to June.

Mama loved spring. Papa liked it because the island was still empty of tourists. But Mama saw color.

"That's wonderful, look! Pink, and that wonderful warm gray. Violet and mauve!" she said.

Mama made Lalo smile.

"Your mother is not trustworthy," he said. "So, just remember your Christmas tree."

Papa laughed. Sophie had helped trim the tree, carefully setting large untidy wads of cotton on one side. Mama wouldn't allow anyone to change it.

"It's Sophie's Christmas too," she said firmly.

Lalo thought it was the ugliest tree he had ever seen, and he said so.

"It is very tasteless," he said admiringly.

"There's some redundancy there," I said, echoing Rebel.

The tree had leaned to one side all through Christmas, finally falling in a heap on New Year's Day, glass balls breaking and the lights going out with a final flash.

A Christmas letter and package had come for Sophie, delivered two weeks late because of windstorms that kept the ferry in port and the planes on the ground. Papa read us the letter.

*Dearest Sophie,*
*I think of you and miss you. Things are better.*
*Love,*
*Mama*

*Things are better.* None of Sophie's mother's letters had ever said that. Each month she wrote, sometimes twice a month, always saying the same things: I love you, I miss you. But no letter had ever said things are better.

Byrd got up and walked to the window, pulling a curtain aside to look out.

"It was a good Christmas with Sophie here," she said, her voice sounding far away and unsteady.

Mama unwrapped the package, a small rubber doll in a red dress. She handed it to Sophie. Sophie turned it over in her hand. She pulled a leg off.

"Baby leg," she said.

She smiled and pulled the other one off.

Mama leaned over and took Sophie in her arms.

Papa looked at me quickly, then went off to work. And winter slipped into spring with those words—*things are better*—always with us, following us like clouds over our heads.

When it came to Mama that it was really, truly spring, she made us bundle up for the beach. Every spring she took her easel and paints to the beach before tourists came. She packed picnic lunches, and we pretended it was warm.

"It's April, love," Mama told Papa cheerfully. "Let's go."

"This is your mother's robust time of year," said Papa grumpily, pulling on his hat with the ear flaps.

"Well, I'm not going," said Byrd. "I'm going to sit by the fire."

"Sophie's going," said Mama slyly.

"That's unfair," said Byrd.

Byrd got up and put on her boots with the fleece lining and her wool hat, and we all went. Papa carried Sophie on his shoulders, Mama carried her paint box. We walked through town.

"Hello, you foolish people!" called Griffey from his sewer truck. "Hello there, Sophie!"

"Hello, Sophie!" yelled Sophie.

Marvella waved from the inn window, watching our procession, and Lalo came out on the porch.

"Is it spring?" he called excitedly. "Wait for me!"

He disappeared and came out wearing the new red wool scarf that Marvella had knitted for him. It wound around his neck several times, another wool barrier from germs, and trailed behind him on the ground.

Lalo saw Papa smiling at it.

"My mother was overcome by knitting during the winter," said Lalo, winding the scarf around his neck one more time. "Totally overcome," he added, peering sideways at me. "I know that's redundant. My mother is redundant."

"You look splendid, dear," said Byrd. "Rather like the cavalry."

She took Lalo's arm and we walked on.

"Besides," she said softly, "that scarf may save us all from freezing."

Old man Brick passed us, his ancient truck lurching. Then we heard a motorcycle. Lalo looked at me as Rebel came down the main street. On the back of his motorcycle was Ms. Minifred, her hair blowing out under her red and white striped helmet. They waved. We waved.

"Hello, Eunice!" Mama called.

Lalo and I stopped walking suddenly.

"Eunice?" I said. "Ms. Minifred's name is Eunice?"

Lalo grinned.

"She rides in beauty, Eunice Minifred does," said Papa, putting his arm around Mama, as Ms. Minifred and Rebel roared down the street.

"Yep," said Lalo, laughing.

"Yep," I said.

"Yep," said Sophie.

The water was blue and green, the sky clear except for high clouds that made me think of Sophie's cotton wads on the Christmas tree. We found a place by a dune, out of the wind that blew the sand along the beach. Byrd sat back, leaning against a driftwood log, Lalo close next to her, the scarf draped around them like a red snake.

"It's too windy for painting," said Mama, taking out her sketchbook.

Papa walked off a bit, looking out over the water. Sanderlings raced the waves, always just ahead of them, their heads bobbing as they fed. On the rocks were purple sandpipers, left over from winter. Black-bellied plovers flew to the beach, settled, then flew off again.

Papa turned and smiled and held out his hand to Sophie. She ran to him, her hat flying off in the wind. Papa picked it up and took her hand. The two of them walked slowly down the beach, the clouds behind them as large as mountains.

"It looks like they're walking into a painting," I said.

Byrd and Mama turned at the same time, watching Papa bend down and point to the sky. Sophie put her hand on his shoulder and looked up. Far away, cormorants flew close to the water in a line. Behind them the ferry moved slowly toward us. Papa sat down with Sophie on his lap. He bent his head and talked to her for a long time. They both looked up at the sky. The wind died then, and the sun came out from behind the big cloud, and there was that sudden silence that comes when the waves stop crashing.

"Oh, my," whispered Byrd.

I watched Mama look at Papa and Sophie. There was a look about her that was half happy, half sad.

"Spring," Mama whispered back.

Ms. Minifred said once that life is made up of circles.

"Life is not a straight line," she said. "And

sometimes we circle back to a past time. But we are not the same. We are changed forever."

I didn't understand what she meant then. I remember steam whistling in the radiator under the window in the school library, and the way Ms. Minifred's hair brushed the side of her face when she leaned forward. But I liked the sound of her words, and I remember saving them for later.

Sophie didn't want to leave the beach, but Papa picked her up, wailing, and we slowly walked back through town. When she stopped crying Papa put her down. Sophie stood there frowning at him, her forehead wrinkled with the effort. After a moment she reached up and took his hand.

"Forgiveness," said Papa to Mama.

The two of them walked ahead of us as the light began to fade from the sky, Sophie's red boots making a slapping sound on the sidewalk. And then, suddenly, Sophie began to shuffle. "Me and My Shadow." We stopped, Mama laughing. People passing by smiled, too, and Papa began to dance with her. Papa smiled at Mama over Sophie's head, and the sky darkened into dusk. Finally, Papa swooped Sophie up in his arms and we began to walk home. We started up the hill to our house. Dry grass crunched under our feet.

And when Lalo and I ran ahead of them through the meadow of dry chickory and meadowsweet, when we climbed up and over the rise to my house, she was sitting in the darkness of the porch. Sophie's mother.

Life is made up of circles.

# Chapter Fifteen

Lalo and I stopped. We both knew. Lalo, as if remembering a cue from the past, moved in front of me. Byrd came up quietly beside us, and I turned to tell her. But she knew too. I could tell by the steady look she gave the woman on the porch and the stillness that came over her face. Byrd lifted her shoulders and pulled her jacket around her, smoothing it over the buttons as if she was preparing for something. Behind us, below the crest of the hill, Mama laughed, and we could hear Papa's voice.

I clenched my teeth. I wanted to turn and call to Papa and Mama to take Sophie away, to turn and run as fast as they could. Lalo knew it, because he took my hand and held it to keep me there.

"Larkin," he whispered.

There was a silence. The woman on the porch didn't move.

"Larkin," he said again. He said it in a way I'd never heard before. It was the saddest sound, as if he was trying to say he knew how bad this was and to protect me at the same time, trying to wrap my name around me like his long wool scarf.

And then we heard the sound of Sophie's high voice. The woman on the porch rose suddenly from the chair and walked to the edge of the porch into the late light of the day. She held on to the porch post, and we all turned as Mama and Papa and Sophie came up the path.

Mama walked ahead of Papa and Sophie, Sophie on Papa's shoulders. Mama walked up to us with a questioning look as we stood there.

"What—?" she began, and then she saw Sophie's mother.

It was like a movie run slowly: Byrd putting out her hand, Mama's face showing the slow recognition, her face slipping, like Byrd's, into a mask that didn't look like Mama anymore; Mama moving away from Byrd, taking a step toward Papa, away from the woman who didn't see the rest of us anymore. All in that moment.

"Sophie," the woman whispered.

Papa stumbled a little, and then he stood still, looking at Sophie's mother. After a moment he walked up to Mama. He stared at her, and then put his arm around Mama. Sophie leaned over, smiling at this, her hands patting Mama's head.

"My baby," the woman said.

And Sophie straightened. She looked over and studied the woman for a moment.

"Not baby," said Sophie.

And on the porch her mother's face slowly crumpled. She burst into tears, sitting on the porch steps, her hands over her face.

Byrd took a breath and moved, but Mama's voice stopped her.

"Sophie?" Mama reached up and took Sophie down from Papa's shoulders. She carried Sophie over to the porch and sat down beside the woman. I looked at Papa and watched the way he looked at Mama. And then Mama said the words that were the hardest to say.

"This is your mama."

I can never forget the small things, the tiny gestures, the look of Mama's eyes, Papa's face, the way Byrd sat so still and careful as if a breeze might topple her. Sometimes these things play over and over in my head like the notes and rhythms of a song.

Our coats hung in the hallway closet. Our boots were lined up in pairs, except for Sophie's. Papa poked at the fire, moved a log, then poked again. He hung the fire poker on a hook, and it fell on the hearth in a clatter that made us all jump. Byrd sat in a straight chair, her legs crossed at the ankles, Mama on the sofa. Sophie's mother stood staring at Sophie, who wore her boots and a sweater Marvella had knitted for her, the too-long sleeves rolled at her wrists. Sophie sat on the floor and slowly began to build a tower with her blocks. Red on blue on green.

"Julia?" Mama said.

Julia. It was hard to think of Sophie's mother with a name. We had always called her Sophie's mother.

Mama held a cup of tea out to her.

"Now," said Mama.

Julia sighed, then looked at Lalo and me standing by the front door.

"Maybe we should talk alone," she said.

Her voice was low and soft. Sophie looked up at her suddenly, her hands stopped above the blocks. *That look.* Does she remember her mother? Does she miss her? I had asked Mama that a long time ago. *That look.* Lalo moved a little beside me, the smallest movement, like a sigh.

"No," said Byrd very quietly, so quietly that we all looked at her. All of us except for Sophie, who stared at her mother.

"Everyone here has been Sophie's family since"— Byrd paused—"since you left her," said Byrd.

Julia winced. She sat down by the fireplace.

"Everyone here has rocked her and read to her and wiped her tears and sung to her. Lalo taught her how to blow a kiss, and sometimes she slept with Larkin. She painted with Lily and she danced with John." Byrd paused. "Everyone here has been her family."

There was silence.

Julia looked at Byrd, and then at Lalo and me, studying us for a moment. She turned back to Byrd.

"That is why I chose you," she said softly.

And then, for the first time, she smiled. Lalo turned his head to look at me. I couldn't look at him, but I knew what his look meant. Julia's smile was Sophie's smile.

Papa sat down next to Mama. He reached over and took her hand. They looked at Julia.

Julia began to speak.

"I watched you last summer, all of you," she said.

Sophie got up from the floor and moved closer to the fire.

"Hot," Julia said almost without thinking.

Sophie looked up.

"Fire is hot," she said.

Julia stared at her.

"Sophie talks," she whispered.

"Sophie talks," whispered Sophie back to her.

Julia swallowed. Tears sat in the corners of her eyes.

"Sophie's father was sick," she whispered. "We knew he would need an operation, and we knew that he would need care all the time. All *my* time. If he didn't die. There was no one else. That was when I saw you."

She stopped then, and looked at Byrd.

"And my parents were not good parents," she said in a flat voice. "I never would have let them have Sophie. Never. I didn't want Sophie to be with strangers. And you didn't feel like strangers."

"You wrote—" began Mama, but her voice broke. "You wrote that things are better."

"Sophie's father will get well," said Julia.

Papa moved on the sofa.

"You took a great risk," he said.

It was the first time he had spoken.

Julia looked at him, then at the rest of us.

"But that is what a mother does," she said.

No one spoke.

I wanted to hate her. I wanted her to go away and leave Sophie with us. I didn't ever want to see her again. Ever. But I couldn't hate her, because in the silence of the room Sophie walked over to her mother. She didn't speak. They stared at each other for a moment. Then Sophie put her hand out and Sophie's mother took it, and Sophie began to move her hand up and down. Something familiar from long ago.

Tears came down Papa's cheeks.

Circles.

The ferry stood at the dock. It looked old and worn in the light of morning, all of its rust and sea-streaked paint showing. The wind blew in gusts, some so harsh that Byrd held on to Lalo's arm. Three cars and an empty flatbed truck went on the ferry, making a lonely clatter on the metal gangplank. A handful of people walked on, turning to wave to the handful on the wharf. Papa held Sophie tightly, and walked away from us, farther down the wharf. Sophie pointed up to the sky. Papa spoke to her, and she smiled.

I saw Griffey, Rollie, and Arthur back by the gas pump looking strange without their instruments. Old man Brick sat in his truck, looking through the windshield. He didn't get out. Lalo's mother and father walked down the sidewalk, and Dr. Fortunato's car drove in and stopped where the wooden wharf began. He opened the door and stood next to it, watching us. Rebel sat on his motorcycle, and Ms. Minifred got off the back. A gust of wind came up, and her hair blew across her face. Without looking at her Rebel handed her his scarf.

Julia turned to Mama.

"Thank you is all there's left to say," she said.

Mama took her hand, then they both looked at Papa.

"John."

Mama said his name softly, but even in the wind he heard.

He stood still for a moment. Then he kissed Sophie. He walked back to us. He handed Sophie to her mother. Byrd reached over and put the necklace with the ruby around Sophie's neck.

Julia turned and walked onto the ferry. Sophie stared at us over her back. Her eyes were solemn. I looked quickly at Papa, and he stared at Sophie as if he were trying to memorize her. Sophie didn't smile. But just before she disappeared inside she reached over Julia's back and held out her hand to Papa. A small fist. Beside me Papa's hand did paper, scissors, back to her. It was then that Sophie smiled.

# Chapter Sixteen

We walked up the hill in silence, through the field, past the pond where the wind sent ripples across the water. Even Lalo didn't talk. The wind caught Byrd's hat once, and Papa grabbed it. He handed it back without words.

The house was cool. The smell of dead ashes hung in the air. Papa went to the fireplace and stood there, looking down as if waiting for the fire to blaze again. Mama took off her hat and leaned against the front door, staring into the room. Byrd bent down and picked up a book. Sophie's book. Byrd straightened.

"We are going to talk now," she said softly.

Papa turned. "Not now," he said. His face had the look of his business face, but his voice was thin, like a thread of smoke.

Mama took off her coat and walked to her studio door.

"You cannot walk away and leave this behind as if it never happened," said Byrd. She paused. "Like the baby."

Mama stopped. Papa stared at Byrd. I stared too. And then the ferry whistle blew, a terrible soft sound behind the closed door. Papa flinched, and in that moment his business look was gone.

It was quiet when the sound ended, and I could hear Lalo breathing beside me.

"*That's* why we're going to talk," said Byrd softly.

Mama's face changed then. She looked transparent, as if all her feelings were there right under her skin. I heard the front door opening and closing, and when I turned Lalo had left.

"Come. Sit down," said Byrd. Her voice had changed, and it sounded almost friendly, like a pleasant invitation.

No one moved.

"I'll sit, then," said Byrd. "I'm old," she added.

Byrd moved to the straight chair by the fireplace. She looked at me.

"If we talk about Sophie, we can talk about Larkin's brother who died. The baby she never saw. The baby with no name."

I walked across the room and sat on the couch.

"Words," Byrd said.

She smiled slightly and I gathered courage from that.

"Even *Sophie* had words," I said.

Papa studied me for a moment, then he looked at Mama across the room. He let out a breath, as if he'd been holding it for a long time. He went over and took Mama's hand.

"Words, Lily," he whispered to her. "Not paint ing. Not dancing. *Words*." Mama was so quiet, like a statue that might break apart if it were touched.

Papa put his arm around her. He looked at me. Then he began to speak.

"His eyes were dark blue, Larkin," he said softly. "So dark, but bright at the same time. Like stars," he whispered.

I stared at Papa. Byrd moved a little beside me.

Mama looked up at Papa. "His hands," she said softly. "His hands had long fingers, like Larkin's. And he had a serious, thoughtful look."

I looked out the window and I could see the distant smoke from the ferry. Then Mama came to sit by me. And in the cool still room, as the ferry took Sophie away, we named the baby William.

It had been warm in the cemetery, the late afternoon sun low in the sky. Light slanted over us and the gravestones, making us all look the same, stones and people. The only sound was the sound of waves on the outer beach, waves one after the other, like heartbeats.

Everyone had come and gone; Griffey and Rollie and the boys who had played a song, Dr. Fortunato, Ms. Minifred and Rebel, who had put a rose on the small gravestone that had WILLIAM engraved on it. And Lalo, who had cried. Byrd had cried, too, when Papa said his words about William.

"I wish I could have danced with him," he said.

Mama had put her arms around Byrd, and they had stood there in that light as everyone went down the hill.

Afterward, we walked home through town, past the stores and houses.

"Will we see her again?" I asked Byrd. "Sophie?"

No one looked surprised. Papa smiled at me. It was easier to talk about Sophie now.

"Yes," said Byrd. "You'll see her again. Sometime."

Mama looked sideways at Byrd and smiled. She stopped.

"Remember walking home with Sophie?" she said. "After we'd been to the beach? Right about there"—she pointed—"and about this time of day, Sophie began to dance."

I walked ahead of them and turned, looking at Byrd, her hair like silver in the light, at Mama and Papa holding hands, at Lalo with his look that seemed to say *I know what you're going to do*. And he did, of course.

I began to do the soft shoe. Papa and Mama stared at me, Papa's eyes widening. Byrd smiled.

*Me and my shadow*
*Strolling down the avenue.*
*Me and my shadow*
*Not a soul to tell our troubles to.*

"I learned," I said. I grinned at the sight of them all, standing there so still and so surprised. And then, for some reason, as I danced I began to cry.

# Summer—
# Ten Years Later

*The memories came all the time now, crowding in, filling her head. They came in mist and clouds, almost revealing what was hidden behind them. Clouds with a face nearly hidden. Clouds.*

*And that face.*

# Chapter Seventeen

We leaned on the boat railing as land came into sight. Birds followed the boat, wheeling above and over it. One herring gull came so close, we could almost touch it. The day was crisp for summer. I turned to look at Sophie as she studied the island. She looked at the cliffs at the far end, then at the town that we could see clearly now, the harbor, the church, the hill where the cemetery was.

Sophie was tall, almost up to my shoulder. Her hair had lost the fair baby color. Now it was the same color as mine. Around her neck was the chain with the red ruby.

Sophie turned to her mother.

"Did you spend a lot of time here?" she asked.

"Only that summer," said Julia. "That summer," she repeated softly, like an echo. Julia looked at me and we smiled.

The boat passed the breakwater and Sophie's hands went up to cover her ears just before the whistle blew.

"You remembered the whistle," I said.

"Did I?" said Sophie. "Sometimes—" Sophie stopped for a moment, then went on. "Sometimes I remember things and I don't know what they mean." Sophie turned and looked at me with the familiar look that made *me* remember her. "I remember a face," she said.

The boat came into the harbor, and Sophie took the newspaper clipping out of her pocket. It was folded over and worn from reading and re-reading. It told of the life, the death, and where the burial would be.

Byrd.

"Will I know them?" asked Sophie. "Will they know me?"

Julia smiled.

"You've seen pictures," she said. "And all those letters." She paused. "Probably yes. Somehow you'll know them."

"They'll know you," I said.

The boat came slowly up to the dock. The lines were tossed and tied. Then we walked down the stairs and onto the landing.

"Do they know I'll be here?" asked Sophie.

I shook my head.

"I didn't know if you'd come," I said.

We walked down the sidewalk, past the stores and houses, and past Lalo's parents' inn. Sophie stopped and looked down at the sidewalk. My heart beat faster.

"You danced here," I said.

Sophie didn't say anything. Then, she reached over and took my hand. We walked along to the grassy place where the cemetery began. Julia stopped and touched Sophie's arm.

"You go ahead," she said.

Sophie looked at her.

"It's all right," said Julia. She smiled. "It will be fine," she said softly.

There were people standing at the top of the hill, their backs to us. We walked up the hill still holding hands. Sophie looked back once, at her mother waiting at the bottom of the hill, looking so small. Then, when we had almost reached the graveside, and we could hear the murmur of low voices, Sophie looked up at the high, thin clouds.

"Mares' tails," she said suddenly. "Mares' tails."

Lalo turned at Sophie's voice. His eyes widened. He grinned at us.

Sophie grinned too. And then, suddenly, Sophie stopped and stared.

*Mares' tails. Mares' tails, and walking in the sand by the water, the wind taking her hat, and the man's whisper in her ear. Mares' tails and the face.*

Papa stood next to a small gravestone with the name WILLIAM engraved on it. He didn't see Sophie. But, just before the minister began to speak Sophie dropped my hand and walked up to Papa. He turned and stared down at her. She smiled at him. She held out her hand.

Rock.

Paper.

Scissors.

# Journey

*For John MacLachlan*

*It is our inward journey that leads us through time—forward or back, seldom in a straight line, most often spiraling.*

—Eudora Welty,
ONE WRITER'S BEGINNINGS


*Photography is a tool for dealing with things everybody knows about but isn't attending to.*

—Emmet Gowin, in
ON PHOTOGRAPHY,
*by Susan Sontag*

*Mama named me Journey. Journey, as if somehow she wished her restlessness on me. But it was Mama who would be gone the year that I was eleven—before spring crashed onto our hillside with explosions of mountain laurel, before summer came with the soft slap of the screen door, breathless nights, and mildew on the books. I should have known, but I didn't. My older sister Cat knew. Grandma knew, but Grandma kept it to herself. Grandfather knew and said so.*

*Mama stood in the barn, her suitcase at her feet.*

*"I'll send money," she said. "For Cat and Journey."*

*"That's not good enough, Liddie," said Grandfather.*

*"I'll be back, Journey," my mother said softly.*

*But I looked up and saw the way the light trembled in her hair, making her look like an angel, someone not earthbound. Even in that moment she was gone.*

*"No, son," Grandfather said to me, his voice loud in the barn. "She won't be back."*

*And that was when I hit him.*

# Chapter One

My grandfather is belly down in the meadow with his camera, taking a close-up of a cow pie. He has, in the weeks since Mama left, taken many photographs—one of our least trustworthy cow, Mary Louise, standing up to her hocks in meadow muck; one of my grandmother in the pantry, reading a book while bees, drawn to her currant wine, surround her head in a small halo; and many of himself, taken with the self-timer device he's not yet figured out. The pictures of himself fascinate him. They line the back of the barn wall in a series of my grandfather in flight, dressed in overalls, caught in the moment of entering the picture, or leaving it;

some with grand dimwitted smiles, his hair flying; one of a long, work-worn hand stretched out gracefully, the only part of him able to make it into the frame before the camera clicks.

Cat gave him the camera in one of her fits of cleanliness.

"I've given up the camera," she yelled, her head underneath the bed, unearthing her life. "I've given up the flute and most everything else. Including meat," she said pointedly. "I have spent the entire afternoon looking into the eyes of a cow, and have become a vegetarian."

"Which cow?" asked my grandmother, not kidding.

Cat gave her a quick look. Grandfather picked up Cat's camera and peered through the lens.

"You tired of this, Cat?"

Cat sighed.

"My pictures are so . . ." She waved her hand to the pile of pictures. "So . . ."

"Boring," Grandfather finished for her.

I felt my face flush with anger, but Cat laughed.

"Take it, Grandpa," she said cheerfully.

Grandfather turned to me.

"Journey?"

"No."

What did he think I'd take pictures of? This farm? I could close my eyes and see it—the spruce trees at the edge of the meadow, the stream cutting through, the stone walls that framed it all. I knew every inch of every acre. What would pictures tell me? And the people. What would pictures tell me of my grandmother, so secretive; my grandfather, tall and blunt?

On Cat's dresser was a picture of our father who had gone away somewhere a long time ago. He was young in the picture, laughing, his eyes looking past the camera, past the place, past me. When I was little, I carried that picture around, trying to remember him, trying to place the picture so that the eyes would look into mine. But they never did. His face was like carved stone, not flesh and blood. And the picture never told me the things I wanted to know. Did he think about Cat and me? Where was he? Would I know him if I saw him?

I turned and the camera clicked: Grandfather's first picture of me. I stared at him angrily, and slowly he lowered the camera and looked at me with a surprised and dismayed expression, as if he'd seen something through the lens that he hadn't expected.

Grandma's voice broke the silence.

"I'll take the flute, Cat. And this."

Grandma had put on the sweatshirt that Mama had given Cat, LIDDIE written across the front in big letters.

"No!" My voice sounded harsher than I meant. "That's Mama's shirt!"

Grandfather put his hand on my shoulder.

"Your mama left it, Journey."

I shook off his hand and stepped away from him.

Grandma stood in the light of the window, her hair all tumbled like Mama's in the barn. I looked at Cat to see if she noticed, but Cat was smiling at Grandma.

"You look wonderful, Gran."

Cat pulled me after her and went to hug Grandma. And Grandfather took a picture that would startle me every time I saw it: not Grandma, her hair tied back with a piece of string, smiling slightly as if she knew the secrets of the world; not Cat, her head thrown back, laughing; but my face, staring into the camera with such fury that even in the midst of the light and the laughter the focus of the picture is me.

# Chapter Two

The first letter that wasn't a letter came in the noon mail. It lay in the middle of the kitchen table like a dropped apple, addressed to Cat and me, Mama's name in the left hand corner.

I'd watched Cat walk up the front path from the mailbox, slowly, as if caught by the camera in slow motion or in a series of what Grandfather called stills: Cat smiling. Cat looking eager. Cat, her face suddenly unfolding out of a smile. She brushed past me at the front door and opened her hand, the letter falling to the table.

"No return address," she said flatly.

My grandmother stirred soup on the stove and

looked sideways at me. After a moment she looked away again.

Grandfather, cleaning his camera lens with lens paper, lifted his shoulders in a sigh, the way he always did when he was about to say something I didn't want to hear.

"I expect—" he began.

Grandma's voice made me jump.

"Marcus!" Then softer. "Let it be."

Cat began to cut carrots at the kitchen counter. My grandfather flinched with each violent stroke.

"I think (thwack) that what Grandpa (thwack) means is that there will be (thwack) money in that envelope. Not words."

Cat stopped and stared down at the counter, the sudden silence like noise filling the room.

"Not the words you want," Cat said softly.

I felt tears behind my eyes. There was something soft and sad in Cat's voice that made me think of Mama.

Grandma stopped stirring the soup, and Grandfather cleared his throat.

"You will be disappointed," he said.

"I'm not disappointed," I said loudly. "I'm not!"

I reached over and tore off one end of the

envelope, blowing inside the way Grandfather always did.

Inside were two small packets of money, the bills fastened with paper clips and a torn piece of paper on each. One said CAT. The other said JOURNEY. The paper clip over my name was bent, as if Mama might have tried to make it right and hadn't. I stared at that paper clip for a long time.

"There are words," I said. My voice rose. "There are words! Our names are there. Our names are words!"

There was silence. The sound of my voice hung in the air between us. Cat turned to face me.

"Journey, you keep the money. Do whatever you want with it."

She began to cut the carrots again, this time calm and steady.

"I'll put it in the bank," I said. Grandma smiled at me from the stove. Grandfather peered at her through his camera and snapped a picture. I stood, suddenly angry, wanting him to stop taking pictures.

"I'll start a travel account!" I shouted.

Surprised, Grandfather put down his camera.

"So that when Mama tells us where she is, Cat

and I can go visit! We'll take a bus . . . or a train. Something fast."

I looked down at the letter in my hand.

"She forgot the return address," I said.

Cat turned at the counter to stare at me.

"She forgot, that's all," I said softly.

Grandma wiped her hands on her apron and came over and put her arms around me. I smelled onion and something like flowers, lilacs maybe, and I burst into tears.

"Ah, Journey," Grandma murmured.

I heard the click of Grandfather's camera.

"Why does he do that?" I asked, my voice muffled in Grandma's shoulder. I leaned back to look at Grandfather. "Why do you do that? Why?"

"Because he needs to," said Grandma softly.

"I don't understand."

"I know," she whispered.

My bedroom was sun-dappled and quiet, the smell of lilacs strong through the open window, mingling with the lily-of-the-valley from under the bush outside.

"Journey?"

The door opened and Grandma stood there with a bowl of soup in one hand, an album in the other. She set the bowl on the table by my bed. Then she opened the album. It was full of pictures, pictures of people I didn't know—men in black suits and white starched shirts and broad-brimmed hats, women in flowered dresses, and children with bows as big as balloons in their hair. Grandma pointed.

"Me," she said, "when I was Cat's age."

In the picture Grandma sat in the garden swing, looking straight at the camera with a great smile on her face. Tables were set up in the garden with food and pitchers and bowls of flowers.

"This was taken on a long-ago Fourth of July." Grandma closed her eyes. "Nineteen thirty, I think. The day I met your grandfather."

"You look happy," I said.

Grandma nodded and looked at the picture.

"The camera knows," she said.

"The camera knows what?"

She turned more pages.

"And here is your mother, same age, same day, but many years later. Grandpa took that picture. He didn't have so fine a camera as now, of course."

In the picture the girl who was my mama sat

behind a table, her face in her hands, looking far off in the distance. All around her were people laughing, talking. Lancie, Mama's sister, made a face at the camera. Uncle Minor, his hair all sunbleached, was caught by the camera taking a handful of cookies. In the background a dog leaped into the air to grab a ball, his ears floating out as if uplifted and held there by the wind. But my mother looked silent and unhearing.

"It's a nice picture," I said. "Except for Mama. It must have been the camera," I said after a moment.

Grandma sighed and took my hand.

"No, it wasn't the camera, Journey. It was your mama. Your mama always wished to be somewhere else."

"Well, now she is," I said.

After a while Grandma got up and left the room. I sat there for a long time, staring at Mama's picture, as if I could will her to turn and talk to the person next to her. If I looked at the picture long enough, my mama would move, stretch, smile at my grandfather behind the camera. But she didn't. I turned away, but her face stayed with me. The expression on Mama's face was one I knew. One I remembered.

*Somewhere else. I am very little, five or six, and in over-*
*alls and new yellow rubber boots. I follow Mama across the*
*meadow. It has rained and everything is washed and shiny,*
*the sky clear. As I walk my feet make squishing sounds,*
*and when I try to catch up with Mama I fall into the*
*brook. I am not afraid, but when I look up Mama has*
*walked away. Arms pick me up, someone else's arms.*
*Someone else takes off my boots and pours out the water. My*
*grandfather. I am angry. It is not my grandfather I want.*
*It is Mama. But Mama is far ahead, and she doesn't look*
*back. She is somewhere else.*

I walked to the window. Birds still sang,
flowers still bloomed, cows still slept in the
meadow, and I ate soup—now cold—as if my mama
hadn't ever gone.

# Chapter Three

Cooper appeared, as he always did, through my bedroom window, this time carrying his baby brother close to his chest in a sling, like a chimpanzee carrying its young. Cooper's face was round and smooth, his brown hair cut even around his face as if his mother might have placed an aluminum bowl over his head. Cooper's face grew even fatter with love when he saw my sister. Cat, sitting on my bed, looking through the photograph album, smiled back at Cooper. She liked him even though he was *my* best friend. She liked him even though he was, in my grandfather's words, "besotted" with her. Almost every year since he was six Cooper had proposed marriage to my sister.

"So?" Cooper raised his eyebrows at me.

I shook my head. Cooper knew that Mama had gone, but he wouldn't ask questions. Questions like Where is she? Why hasn't she written a letter? Why did she go? *Who's to blame here?*

I looked up, startled at my own thought, half afraid I'd spoken out loud, but Cat and Cooper were looking at the baby.

The baby, Emmett, reached his small hand out to Cat, the movement jerky, as if his head wasn't telling his hand how. Cat, smiling, put out her finger, and the baby took it, a sudden contented look settling like silk over his face.

Cooper smiled down at Emmett.

"I've got him for a whole hour while Mama weeds the garden," he said, happily untangling Emmett from the sling. "To shape or ruin his lima-bean brain. What shall it be?"

Emmett leaned back against Cooper and stared at me, as if waiting for an answer, his eyes all dark-wet and wise, and so direct that after a moment I looked away.

"He looks like you, Cooper," said Cat.

"We all look alike," said Cooper. "The whole family, down through the ages, over prairie and sea, desert and mountain. You could toss all our pictures up in the air, and when they came down they'd *all* look like me."

Cat laughed and the baby laughed, too, making us all laugh.

"Well, I don't look like anyone," I said. "Anyone that I know."

Cat scrambled over the bed to pick up the album, turning the pages. Cooper pointed suddenly.

"Is that you, Cat? In the garden?"

Cat was quiet.

"No," she said slowly, "that's Mama. Mama a long time ago."

"Oh." There was a pause, and Cooper looked at me uncomfortably. "It's just that . . ."

"We look so much the same," finished Cat.

She turned back in the album.

"There. That's who I look like!"

It was Grandma's picture in the garden swing. With the smile. Very carefully Cat took the picture out of the album and walked to the mirror. She held the picture up in front of her and smiled.

"There. You see?"

Cooper and I stood behind her, the baby grinning at us all in the mirror.

"Yes," said Cooper. "I do."

Cat looked at me, waiting.

"Yes," I said. It was as if we all stood there, taking a strange oath, in front of a girl with light-touched hair and another who looked the same but not the same in the picture and now had gray hair tied back with a string.

"But," I couldn't help adding, "you look like Mama, too."

Cat's smile became set and her eyes narrowed, and then the baby gave a sudden excited leap in Cooper's arms, and Grandfather stood behind us.

"Ah," he said to the baby. "Look who's come for a visit. Hello, Cooper."

Grandfather took the camera from around his neck and handed it to me. He held out his arms, and Emmett went to him happily, grabbing for his glasses. Laughing, Grandfather took off his glasses and held them out for Cooper to take, and in that moment I held the camera up to my eyes to hide my surprise. Without his glasses my grandfather's face changed; sharp places became softer. Through the camera I could see the wrinkles at the corners of his eyes that made his eyes less hard; his face smoothed out. He looked younger. *He looked* . . . without thinking I pressed the button and the shutter clicked. Grandfather looked up.

"I'm sorry," I said. "I didn't mean to do that."

"No, no, Journey." He smiled at me and sat down on the bed with the baby. "You can take all the pictures you want."

Grandfather sat Emmett on his knees and took his hands.

"Trot, trot to Boston;
Trot, trot to Lynn . . ."

Emmett bounced and grinned. I held the camera up to my face, my eyes closed.

*Trot, trot to Boston;*
*Trot, trot to Lynn;*
*Watch out, little boy,*
*Or you'll fall in.*

*We are in the garden, the light slanting through the trees. Tall flowers—hollyhocks—are nearby, blooms against the barn. Up and down I go, my eyes fastened on white buttons against a blue shirt. The smell of summer fills the air, and voices rising and falling, and laughter.*

*Watch out, little boy,*
*Or you'll . . .*

*My eyes go up from the shirt button to the neck.*

*But there is no face.*

". . . fall in!"

Cooper and Cat laughed; my eyes opened, and I looked through the viewfinder at Grandfather and at Emmett falling back between his knees, their faces in identical expressions—eyes wide, mouths in an O. The baby's laughter fell like sunlight across the room, and as I pressed the button I wished for a way to save that sound, too.

And then Grandfather stood up and put on his glasses again. Slowly I lowered the camera. The baby crawled on the floor. Cat was turning the pages of the photograph album. Cooper yawned. Everything had changed.

Grandfather ran his fingers through his hair, looking over my head into the mirror behind me. I turned and our eyes met. I frowned and he frowned, imitating me, but I wouldn't smile. I took the camera from around my neck and handed it to him.

"Things don't look the same through the camera," I said. "Not the way they are in real life."

Putting the camera strap around his neck, he paused, then straightened.

"Sometimes." He tilted his head to one side and spoke to himself in the mirror. "And sometimes pictures show us what is really there."

"How? How can that be?" I asked.

Grandfather lifted his shoulders in a familiar way, then said something unlike him.

"I don't know, Journey. Maybe that is why people take pictures. To see what is there."

Cat shut the photograph album with a snap, like an exclamation point at the end of a sentence. Emmett on the floor began to fuss, and I bent down to pick him up. He looked at me closely, then with a sigh he put his arms around my neck and lay his head down. My heart seemed to beat faster with the feel of it.

"What do you mean, 'to see what is there'?" I asked after a moment, but when I turned around, Grandfather had gone.

"What does he mean?" I asked Cat.

She didn't answer. Instead, she handed me a photograph. It was old, very old and grainy, as if taken through water or sand or wind. In the picture there was a boy holding the reins of a horse. Plowed fields spread out behind him, furrows as straight as train tracks. The horse nuzzled the boy's pocket, as if there might be sugar cubes there, or an apple; but the boy stared into the camera with a face so familiar that I caught my breath.

"Boy," said Cooper beside me, "that could be you, Journey."

"Eee," said Emmett, echoing Cooper.

"Is that a picture of Papa?" I asked Cat.

Cooper snorted.

"Even I know who that is."

Emmett, stirring in my arms, turned to stare at me as if he knew, too.

"Two of a kind," said Cat.

I saw the face in that picture every day in the mirror. And I had just seen that face through the camera.

The picture was of my grandfather.

# Chapter Four

It is late June, the longest day of the year, Grandma tells me, and the hottest so far. Grandfather and I argue all the way to the car. Actually, Grandfather calls it a "dialogue" we're having. I call it a fight. We fight because he wants me to drive to town.

"I don't know how," I tell him loudly, following him to the driveway.

"You'll learn."

"I don't want to learn."

"You'll be glad someday."

"Why?"

"I'm an old man. If I die in back of the wheel one day you can drive."

My sister, surrounded by books in the backseat in case she gets bored, laughs.

I throw her a look that makes her laugh more.

"I'm only a little boy," I plead.

"Then drive like a little boy," says Grandfather.

The subject is closed, but not before Grandfather tries to take another family picture. In the distance waves of shimmery heat rise off the fields, but Grandfather doesn't care. He sets his camera on a fence post and places us by his car. He makes Grandma come out of the house to pretend she is going to town too.

"Get a hat, Lottie," he calls to her.

Grandma puts on her straw hat with the cloth strawberries and grumbles all the way down the path to the car.

"Look fetching, Lottie," he tells Grandma as he leans down to peer through the camera.

"I'm not an actress, Marcus," says Grandma sharply. "I am a hot, old woman."

"You are a fetching hot, old woman," says Grandfather, making Grandma laugh.

Beside me, Cat wipes the sweat off her forehead. Grandfather's car is already hot; the black surface gleams in the sun.

"Why are we doing this?" I ask loudly.

"The timer is set!" calls Grandfather, ignoring me. "Ready? Ten . . . nine . . . eight . . ."

"Why?" I ask Cat, my teeth clenched.

Cat elbows me gently, and we watch Grandfather begin to run to the car. Grandma licks her lips.

"Four," chants Grandfather, standing tall and trying, I know, to look stately.

"Three," we all say together, our smiles set.

Above us is the droning noise of a small airplane.

"Don't look up!" yells Grandfather, but he does, and we can't help looking, too.

Not one of us hears the soft whirring sound of the shutter clicking.

***

"Oh, Marcus," said Grandma, "it's just . . ." She stopped.

"Lottie," said Grandfather, his lips tight. "I love you dearly, and we've been married for what seems like a hundred and fifty years, but you know there is no such thing as 'just a picture.'"

They looked at each other, and Grandma touched his arm.

"I know," she said.

"Take another," I said, hoping he would forget teaching me to drive the car. "I'm really sorry," I added, and when I said it I realized that I *was* sorry.

Grandfather waved his hand.

"Never mind. Let's get going. I've got rolls of film to drop off and pictures to pick up. I've got things to get in town."

"Things?" asked Grandma. "What things?"

"Things," said Grandfather, moving toward the car. "Photo things. Come on, Journey. Drive."

Grandfather gets in the passenger seat and waits as I climb behind the wheel. There are no seat belts because Grandfather's car is so old. It has scratchy seats and huge fenders. It has a running board. I have never seen another car like his car. My sister says they are extinct. Grandma calls it the passenger pigeon.

I start the car. I know about the clutch and the brake because I can drive a tractor. But Grandfather's car is different, and we lurch off, Grandfather bracing himself with one hand, hanging on to the roof strap with the other, Cat laughing in the backseat.

The moment we get out of sight of the farm my grandfather takes out his camera and hangs out the window, and suddenly I know that he wants me to drive so he can take pictures as we move. I know that if we are in a car crash, Grandfather will photograph it as it happens.

"Keep it steady," says Grandfather, and we pass Millie Bender's parents' fruit stand. Out of the corner of my eye I see a blur of watermelon and peaches, strawberries and Mrs. Bender sitting under a striped umbrella.

We pass a cornfield filled with crows.

"Hey!" yells Grandfather, and the crows rise up in a flapping of wings above us. He leans out backward and aims the camera to the sky.

I laugh.

"Look!" I cry, suddenly excited.

Cooper rides toward us, recognizing the car. He stares at it, about to raise his arm in a wave, when he sees it's me driving. His jaw drops.

"Quick!" I shout. "Take the picture!"

Grandfather leans over me, and he snaps the picture just as Cooper's bicycle begins to wobble. I look in the rearview mirror and watch Cooper watching us.

"You know," I say after a moment, "I bet the picture of us all looking up at the airplane will be fine."

Grandfather looks at me.

"I think you're right, Journey," he says.

"Two of a kind," says Cat.

# Chapter Five

Summer rains came, soft at first, with mists that lay like lace over the meadows. When the sky grew darker and the rain steady, Grandma sent us out to gather peonies. Grumbling, we carried dripping pink and white armfuls into the house, filling all the pitchers we could find and a washtub in the kitchen. The smell filled the house, and so did the ants that crawled down from the blooms, crisscrossing the house like sightseers.

Grandfather, restless, lurked through the hallways, taking pictures with the new flash attachment bought in town and breaking into sudden dances of ant-stomping. Blasts of light popped everywhere until Grandma ran out of patience.

"I have spots in front of my eyes, Marcus! I can't read! Go away. Be a farmer."

Grandfather was insulted.

"I am a farmer who takes pictures," he said haughtily. Then he brightened. "I am a photographer-farmer."

Grandma, only a little amused, banished him to the barn, where I watched him take cow close-ups until the cows, bothered by the lights, showed him their backsides.

"Maybe the chickens," he muttered.

I stood behind Grandfather, trying to see what he saw through the camera. Then I walked to the back of the barn where his pictures hung, looking again at the familiar ones of Grandma and Cat and me. There were new ones, too—Grandma smiling from the stove, and one of Cat hoeing in the garden with a fierce look, the hoe poised above the soil as if she might be killing a black snake. And then I saw it—the picture I had taken of Grandfather with Emmett on his knees, Emmett's mouth opened, light from the window around them both. The edges were blurred and soft, as if it were a painting. Or a memory. *Trot, trot to Boston*. For a moment I felt like I was Emmett, sitting on someone's knees. Someone who sang to me. I stared, goose bumps coming up on my arms. I stepped back to bend down to see the picture better and bumped up against Grandfather standing behind me.

"You moved the camera," he said. "That's why the edges are fuzzy."

I nodded.

"It's not a good picture, I guess."

"Journey," said Grandfather, his voice soft, "it is a wonderful picture."

"But I moved the camera."

"You did. See how it looks like Emmett and I are the only ones there, how we look like we're wrapped in a cocoon, away from the rest of the world? See how the edges frame us?"

Grandfather's voice rose with excitement, and I smiled even though I didn't want to.

"Well," I said, embarrassed and pleased. "Well, it's not perfect."

"Perfect!" Grandfather almost spit out the word. His face softened. "What is perfect? Journey, a thing doesn't have to be perfect to be fine. That goes for a picture. That goes for life." He paused. "Things can be good enough."

I stared at Grandfather, then at my picture. After a moment I felt Grandfather move behind me.

"Grandfather?"

"Yes, Journey."

I turned. Grandfather was standing at the door of the barn, rain pouring off the roof behind him. His old dark green poncho floated from his shoulders like a king's cape.

I swallowed hard.

"Do you think that Mama left because things weren't good enough? Do you think that *I* wasn't . . ."

"No!" Grandfather spoke loudly, his eyes dark. "No," he said, softer. He made a move toward me, then stopped. "Do you know that I tell you the truth? Even when you don't want to hear it?"

I nodded.

"Which? Yes that I tell you the truth or yes that you don't want to hear it?"

I was silent, suddenly remembering that once in this barn he had told me that Mama would not come back. That was not true. I knew that was not true. "Sometimes," I said softly. "Sometimes you tell me the truth."

Grandfather pursed his lips.

"Well, this is an important truth, Journey. It is not . . ." His voice grew louder. "It—is—not—your—fault."

There was a pause, then slowly his face changed, and I knew somehow that we were thinking the same thing. But of course Grandfather said it.

"You need someone to blame, Journey? Is that it?"

I backed up a step.

"Well, it's not Mama's fault," I said stubbornly.

Grandfather sighed.

"No, I can see that you can't blame Liddie. But that's all right. That's all right."

We stared at each other for a moment; then I turned to look at the picture of him and Emmett again.

"I remember things," I said. "I remember 'Trot, trot to Boston.'" I turned to look at him. "I do."

Grandfather smiled faintly.

"I'm not surprised you remember. But you were very little. You wanted to hear that rhyme over and over and over." His voice trailed off.

I picked up Grandfather's camera and looked at him through the viewfinder, standing there with his poncho and rain hat.

"I remember," I said, snapping the picture just before Grandfather's smile faded, "that I sat on my papa's lap. I remember the button on his shirt. And he sang to me and held my hands. And he wouldn't let me fall. He and Mama kept me safe and took care of me until . . ."

I put the camera down and stared at it.

*Until you made them go away.*

The words were unspoken, but when I looked up again, I might just as well have said them out loud by the look on Grandfather's face.

"Where are the pictures?" I asked.

"What?" asked Grandfather. "What pictures?"

"The pictures of Papa and Mama and me. And Cat. When we were babies like Emmett? When I was on Papa's knees?"

Grandfather looked down at the floor.

"There weren't many," he said.

"I don't need many."

Grandfather sighed.

"They're gone," he said.

*Gone.*

"You mean Mama took them?" I asked.

Grandfather took a deep breath and looked me in the eye.

"The truth?"

My skin prickled.

"Yes. Did she take them?"

"No, Journey," said Grandfather. "Your mama tore them up."

# Chapter Six

"I don't believe you're sick," says Cat, standing over my bed like an umpire over home plate. "And if you are sick, you're glad of it. You like us to bring you soup and ginger ale."

"I have a sore throat," I tell her, pulling the covers under my chin.

"Let's see," says Cat, trying to pry my mouth open.

I can hear Grandma in the kitchen practicing scales on the flute.

"I have a temperature, too," I say.

"How many blankets do you have here? One, two, three, a quilt, a bedspread. Journey, you've got five blankets, and it's summer! You may turn into a butterfly."

"Cat, Mama tore up our pictures."

"Yes."

"You knew? Why am I the last to know anything?"

"You know things, Journey. You just don't want to believe them. You believe what you want."

Cat, in a sudden motion, whips my covers off.

"Cat!"

She lets the window shade snap up, and sun clatters into the room. I put my hands over my eyes.

"You're not sick, Journey," says Cat, standing at the window. "You're hiding out."

Grandma was surprised to see me dressed.

"Journey, are you feeling better?"

"Cat made me get up."

Grandma smiled. She put her flute on my bureau.

"Cat is a woman of action. She doesn't believe much in introspection."

"Introspection?"

Grandma sat on my bed.

"What you've been doing in here the past two days. Thinking, mostly about yourself."

I looked up quickly to see if this was an insult, but Grandma was looking out to the garden, where Cat was hoeing between the rows.

"Cat believes that if she keeps busy all the things that bother her will go away," said Grandma.

"Does that work?"

Grandma turned to look at me.

"Not entirely. No more than thinking. But you will notice," she added, "that my garden is twice the size it was last year."

I looked out at the rows of lettuce and radishes, the fernlike tops of carrots. Grandma had turned up more grass this year, and she had even planted corn that stood stomach high to me. We watched Cat finish a row, then stand back, wiping the back of her hand over her forehead. She lifted her shoulders suddenly, then began working again.

Grandma leaned against the window frame and looked out, past Cat in the garden, past the meadows. Her face looked sad. *She misses Mama, too.* Aunt Lancie and Uncle Minor had moved away, and they visited sometimes. But Mama had stayed on to live with Grandma. Mama and Papa. And Mama was the youngest.

"We all do the best we can, you know," said

Grandma. "Your sister and I garden ourselves into madness." She looked at me. "You think yourself into a sore throat." She sighed and gestured toward the barn. "And your grandfather takes pictures."

Grandfather, his camera around his neck, was prowling along the stone wall outside, his eye on Cat. Through the window we could see him say something. We could see Cat turn with a surprised look, like a deer startled in the garden, as Grandfather took her picture.

"Watch now, Journey," Grandma whispered. "That old buzzard is going to take a picture of us."

"How do you know?" I whispered back. "He didn't even look this way."

"Oh yes he did. I saw his eyes roll to the side. I am the smartest woman in this room."

"Why are we whispering?" I whispered.

Grandma began to laugh, and she put her arm around me. I smiled, and we both looked out. Suddenly Grandfather whirled and aimed his camera at us in the window.

"Such a noodle," said Grandma, laughing as he took our picture. She wiped her eyes with a handkerchief.

"Grandma?"

"What?"

"Why did Mama do it? The pictures?"

Grandma shrugged.

"I can't speak for Liddie. I never could, Journey. And it wouldn't be fair to you if I did."

"Then," I said, "I'll have to ask her when I see her."

Grandma looked at me, a quick look. She reached out to smooth my hair.

"I hope you get to do that, Journey. I really do."

Grandma went to the dresser and picked up her flute.

"He shouldn't have told me," I said suddenly. "Grandfather shouldn't have told me about the pictures."

"But, Journey," Grandma said softly, "you asked him." Grandma paused for a moment to look at the old picture of Mama that leaned against the dresser.

"Funny, isn't it, how we are sometimes angry at the wrong person."

She gave her head a little shake, as if shaking off a fly, then she went out the door.

"You," I whispered to the picture. "I *could* have a sore throat. I *could* have a temperature."

I leaned my elbows on the dresser and peered into Mama's face.

"Do you hear me?"

# Chapter Seven

And then the cat came. After the rains, when Grandfather and I were silent and uneasy with each other, and the lawn grew too long, and June bugs threw themselves against the lamplit screens, I heard the soft thump as the cat jumped up to my sill. The cat stared at me, its face like a pansy, and then, without claws, it lifted a paw and hit the window screen. The tiniest of sounds. Very carefully I lifted the screen, and the cat walked inside, across my desk, and settled on my bed as if it were home. As if the cat were someone come back in disguise. Almost at once the cat slept.

Slowly I backed out of the room, racing to the kitchen.

"Cat?"

Grandma looked up.

"Your sister's not here, Journey. Do you want something?"

No. I knew how Grandma felt about cats.

Behind her, Grandfather was standing, leaning against the counter, stirring coffee.

"No, Grandma, thanks. Good night."

"Good night then," said Grandma, threading a needle in the light.

I looked at Grandfather, and he looked back at me, taking a sip of his coffee, his eyes narrowed against the steam. He turned his head to one side, as if he were getting a different view of me. I lifted my shoulders, took a breath, and beckoned to him, putting a finger to my lips. His eyebrows rose. After a moment he put down his coffee, silently following me down the hallway to my room.

"What is it?" he said at my bedroom door.

"Look," I whispered, pulling his arm. I pointed.

"Oh, my," whispered Grandfather. He smiled. "Look at that, all tuckered out."

Slowly he walked to the bed. The cat stretched, looked up at him, then curled up again.

"Whose cat is it?" asked Grandfather.

I was silent.

Grandfather quickly looked down at me.

"Journey," he warned, "no. You know your grandma is not fond of cats. She loves her birds."

"I love this cat," I said. "He tapped on my window screen. I think he's mine."

"Do not," said Grandfather, whispering fiercely, "do not name this cat."

I knew the family rule. Do not name an animal or you'll have to take care of it. If you name it, it's yours.

"He tapped on my screen and walked right in and went to sleep," I went on, "just like he lives here. And he does."

I put out my hand and stroked the cat, and he put his paws around my hand, hugging me to him.

"See?" I whispered.

Grandfather bent down.

"There's blood here, Journey. See, a little trail on the floor."

Grandfather ran his hands over the cat, who peered at him through slit eyes.

"Here it is. A little cut on his foot."

Grandfather took out his handkerchief and blotted the cat's left paw. Suddenly the cat reached over and took Grandfather's finger in his teeth. I held my breath as Grandfather and the cat stared at each other. After a moment Grandfather smiled.

"You are something," he said to the cat, and to prove it, the cat let go of his finger, turned over, and went back to sleep.

"What is going on here?"

Grandma's voice made Grandfather jump. The cat didn't move.

"Oh, for heaven's sake, Marcus!"

My sister appeared suddenly behind Grandma. Her face lighted up when she saw the cat.

"Oh!" She turned to me. "Have you named him yet?"

"Marcus!" said Grandma warningly, her lips pressed tightly together.

"Now, Lottie," said Grandfather, "this is an injured animal. We have to be humane here."

"You know how I feel about cats," said Grandma. "And cats are not humane to birds."

"We'll put a bell on him," I said. "Two bells, Grandma! Please!" Grandma's face was stern. I turned to Grandfather. "I need this cat."

My own words startled me, and Grandfather cleared his throat.

"Actually, Lottie, it's unfortunate, I know, but Journey has named him already."

I stared at Grandfather. Grandma saw my surprise.

"Really," she said, folding her arms across her chest. "And what would that name be?"

"Yes," said Grandfather. His eyes roamed the room. "His name is . . ." Grandfather looked at the vase of peonies by the window. "His name is Bloom, isn't that what you called him, Journey?"

"Yes." I nodded.

"Oh, push," said Grandma, half smiling, "you just made that up, old man. You might just as well have said Peony."

"Lottie," said Grandfather, "Journey knows that Peony is no name for a cat."

The screen opened, and Cooper poked his head in.

"I saw the lights."

He climbed in, closing the screen behind him, and then he saw the cat. Cooper peered at Grandfather, at my sister leaning against the wall, and at Grandma with her arms still folded. Finally he looked at me.

"Of course you named him," he said, making Grandfather's lips twitch.

"Bloom," I said.

"I'll get the camera," said Grandfather.

As it turned out the name Bloom fit the cat well. In Grandma's words, Bloom was about to burst into flower. In Grandfather's words, "He's a she, she's pregnant. You're going to be a papa."

Grandma pretended anger at the idea of more than one cat. But I thought that she'd known the moment she first saw Bloom. And Bloom, if she loved anyone, loved Grandma. She ran to her in the morning with a small, eager sound of welcome. She brought sodden and well-chewed mice to the doorstep, waiting proudly for Grandma to run through all her words of disgust. She sat beside Grandma on the living room couch at night, watching Grandma closely.

We tied a bell on Bloom so she wouldn't catch birds, but Bloom would not wear it, managing to chew it off. Late into the night we heard the sound of Bloom batting it up and down the hallways of the house before she came to my bed to sleep. But as far as I knew, Bloom never caught a bird. If she did, she never brought it to Grandma's doorstep.

"She knows," said Cat admiringly.

"She's the most intelligent cat I've ever known," added Cooper, who had never known any cat well. "Intelligent enough to know your grandma would kill her and toss her on the compost heap."

I knew better. I knew that Grandma and Bloom had a secret life of their own. Once, hidden in the pantry, I heard what Bloom heard each day from Grandma.

"Oh no, you filthy little cannibal! Take that mouse away, you wretch!" Then whispered, "You are one splendid girl. The best in all the world. Would you like a treat?"

One morning I borrowed Grandpa's camera and stalked them in the garden, and I took a picture of Grandma leaning over the onions to whisper to Bloom, Bloom's tail high, her face lifted to Grandma's, almost a kiss.

Days later, when Grandfather saw the picture he grew very quiet, and when I looked up at him his eyes were wet. He pinned the picture on the wall of the barn, and we stood next to each other, not speaking for a long time. Then we had the shortest conversation of our lives so far.

"Lottie needs that cat," said Grandfather.

I nodded.

"The camera knows," I said.

# Chapter Eight

The days grew hot and Bloom grew fat. Humid air hung heavy as parlor drapes in the house, but still no letters came—only small packets of money with envelopes leaving a postmark path I couldn't follow. Grandma took the fruit out of her crystal bowl in the dining room, and Bloom climbed in happily to keep cool. Grandfather groused ("She doesn't even let me *wash* that bowl"), but when Grandma left he set the table with all the china and silver, candles burning, and took a picture of Bloom lolling in the bowl like a queen. Then he handed me the camera, and I took a picture of them both—Bloom in the bowl and Grandfather at the head of the table, the candle flames reflected in their eyes.

During the hot days Grandfather was seized by picture taking. He took a picture of Cat and me, up to our necks in the brook, and Cooper, his white wrinkled feet thrust up between our faces. He took Grandma in the hammock under the tulip tree, playing her flute to Bloom, above her on a branch. He made me drive the John Deere through the hay-field as he perched dangerously over the cutter, photographing the blades as they turned.

"If I fall," he yelled over the noise of the engine, "grab the camera!"

And he maddened the chickens, trying to take a still life of eggs in the henhouse.

But it was the family pictures that consumed him and drove us into hiding. We would hear him call "Everyone!" innocently, and we would run to different parts of the house—Grandma into the pantry, closing the door after her, Cat under her bed, and me to the attic. But he always found us. Once, we posed in the doorway of the barn, nicely framed, but a chicken flew past us. Even Bloom caught the tone and would streak past us into the nearest room or behind the curtains. Or, just that once, into Mama's room.

That's why it was Bloom who found them.

Under the bed in the room we never entered, in the room that Mama had stripped of herself, Bloom hid next to the box, waiting for us to find her.

"What is this?" said Cat, lying down next to the bed. "Come out, Bloom."

I lay down, too, lifting the dust ruffle. Bloom batted at my hand, then jumped into a box. I reached out and pulled the box out from under, Bloom crouched down inside.

Behind us was a noise. Grandfather held Grandma's arm as if she were his captive.

"Come on, now, I've caught her. Just one picture."

And then Bloom jumped out of the box.

And Grandfather's face changed.

Inside the box were torn pictures, hundreds of them. Bits and pieces of faces and arms and bodies; slices of scenes, of sky and flowers; a door, a porch here; the barn, the face of a cow peering over the fence. *A baby's hand.*

I stood up. Grandma put her hand on my shoulder.

"She didn't throw them away," I said, my voice a whisper.

"Doesn't look like it," said Grandfather stiffly.

He exchanged a look with Grandma.

"Well," said Cat, getting up and dusting off her pants. "She sure did in our family. Didn't she?"

No one spoke. Then Cat looked up at Grandfather and Grandma. "It looks like murder to me."

*Murder*. The word washed over me. It did look like a killing. Cat was right. Inside that box were people: Cat and Mama and Papa. And me. Was that baby's hand my hand?

I picked up the box and looked at Cat. Her face was pale. Tears sat at the corners of her eyes.

"I'll fix this, Cat," I said to her. "I'll tape these pictures back together again."

"Oh, Journey," began Grandma.

But Grandfather stopped her.

"It's all right, Lottie. Journey's got a right to these pictures."

He reached into the box and cradled a handful of torn pictures in his hand. Pieces slipped through his fingers like water.

"It's Journey's past," he said.

Morning has come and gone, and afternoon, too. A standing lamp shines down, a yellow pool on the pictures. Faces stare up at me, and a dog I don't remember or I've forgotten, and Cat's face when she was seven or eight. But it is the baby's hand. Where is the face? And where is the picture of the man who holds him?

For a long time I work alone, sorting and shifting picture pieces like a giant puzzle. But I can piece together only a few. Not the ones I want. Cat comes to crouch down, but she only looks. Grandma comes to bring me dinner on a plate, and later Grandfather stands above me so he won't cast a shadow. He leans down for a moment, picking up a piece, then putting it back. Then, without a sound, he is gone.

There is moonlight at the windows when something, a movement in the room, startles me. Bloom walks across the pictures, and I look up and Cooper is sitting in a chair by the window. He is wearing a strange cowboy hat, too small, that sits high on his head. We stare at each other.

"Cooper," I say, my voice soft, "I will put all these pictures back together, and everything will be all right."

Cooper is silent. I look up at him.

"It will," I say. "It will," I whisper.

# Chapter Nine

*I am dreaming. I always know when I am dreaming because I can fly. I fly over the farm, over the blueberry barren, over the barn and house. I fly over Grandfather in the field, and when I call down to him he raises his camera and takes a picture of me with my wings all warm. Then I fly down a road. The road turns into a map, and the map is large with all the roads marked, and I follow all the towns one by one by one. When I try to call down again, my voice has changed to a bird's voice. And no one looks up.*

I woke, sweating, with early light coming in the window. I sat up, looking over to the chair in the corner, and then I remembered that Cooper had left, long ago. Long ago, after we had worked, and Cooper had sat back suddenly and told me that it was impossible. That was the word he used, *impossible*. That I couldn't patch all the pictures together because there were so many; more than I had thought. *Look,* he had said to me, *some of these pictures are very old; here is part of your grandmother's face when she was very little. Like the picture in the swing. Remember?*

My grandma's face. *She had even torn up my grandma.*

And I told Cooper his cowboy hat looked stupid. And he left.

And I knew Mama was never coming back.

I got up and looked out the window. Cooper's bike leaned against the house, and I half expected to see him there, too, but I knew he had walked home alone through the fields in the dark.

Behind me the lamp was still on, its pale yellow light spilling out over the pictures. I bent down and picked up the pieces, trying not to look at the faces of the people as I filled the box and put it in my closet. Bloom appeared to rub her face against my arm. With a small sound, she jumped into the box and lay there, looking up at me through tired eyes.

"The box is yours, Bloom," I said. "You found it, after all."

And I climbed out the window, very quietly so as not to wake anyone, and began to pedal Cooper's bicycle down the road to his house. I didn't get very far when I began to cry.

Cooper's house was white clapboard with a cement sidewalk, his mother's narrow lines of alternating white petunias and red salvia on either side. I thought of Grandma's growing garden of flowers and vegetables, getting larger as the days passed. Cooper's mother didn't like to garden.

"If God had wanted us to garden, he would have had plots all dug up, waiting for us. And he wouldn't have created weeds, either," she once said.

I wheeled the bicycle up the walk. I was not surprised to see Cooper sitting on the front porch in a white metal chair. I was not surprised, either, that he still wore his cowboy hat.

"Thanks for bringing my bike," he said.

"I'm sorry. What I said about your hat," I told him.

Cooper nodded. I sat down next to him.

We looked out over the neat yard.

"You been crying?" asked Cooper, not looking at me.

"Yes."

After a moment Cooper shrugged his shoulders like Grandfather.

"Well, then," he said, "let's go in. Mrs. MacDougal is making breakfast."

Cooper called his mother Mrs. MacDougal. So did Mr. MacDougal. I expected that one day soon Emmett would ask for his bottle please, Mrs. MacDougal.

In the kitchen Cooper's mother was making pancakes. Emmett sat in his high chair, smears of banana and applesauce across his face and up his arms to his elbows. His hair was stuck to his scalp with pancake syrup. Food lined the creases of his neck like putty.

"He's learning to feed himself," explained Mrs. MacDougal, putting a plate in front of me. "You'll have some breakfast, Journey?"

Emmett grinned at me, banana oozing around his two front teeth.

"Just a little, please," I said, and Cooper laughed.

"Mr. MacDougal!" called Cooper's mother.

"I've eaten, Mrs. MacDougal!" answered Cooper's father from upstairs. But soon he exploded into the room in his work clothes and kissed Emmett, then Cooper, then Mrs. MacDougal, then me. I was startled, trying to remember the last time someone had kissed me. The kiss was warm on my forehead, and I bent my head down to finish my pancake.

Cooper's house was filled with MacDougals—pictures on the refrigerator and above the doorway. After we ate I followed Cooper into the dining room, where his great-grandparents hung over the sideboard. In the living room were pictures of Cooper as a baby, plump as a plum; Mr. and Mrs. MacDougal before they were married; and newer pictures of Emmett, all cleaned up and looking wise. I walked from room to room with Cooper, watching his life on the walls.

"Grandfather says pictures show us the truth sometimes," I said.

Mrs. MacDougal stood in the doorway, watching us.

"Sometimes, maybe. But do you see that picture of me, there on the piano?"

I picked up the picture, framed in silver. Mrs. MacDougal was young, her mother and father standing formally behind her, her brothers flanking her protectively.

"Don't we look the perfect family?"

I smiled at her and nodded.

"Well, my brother Fergus, there on the left, was pinching the devil out of me when that picture was taken. He did that all my life. He still does."

I peered at the picture closely, searching for a look that told me this. But there were only smiles.

"Sometimes," said Mrs. MacDougal, "the truth is somewhere behind the pictures. Not in them."

In the kitchen, still in his high chair, Emmett began to fuss.

"Ah, well," said Mrs. MacDougal, "I'd better go hose him down." She turned. "It's early, Journey. Do Marcus and Lottie know where you are?"

"I'm going to ride him home on my bike, Mrs. MacDougal," said Cooper.

We ride up the dirt road, me sitting on the seat, my legs out, Cooper pedaling in front of me. I hold on to his waist, and we pass fields and meadows and cows; we pass Weezer, the Moodys' old dog, who makes a show of chasing us.

"Weezer, Weezer," chants Cooper, and Weezer stops, stunned by the sound of his name, just before he runs into the mailbox.

We pass the Fullers' horse farm, and the foals race along the fence, sending up little dust clouds when they stop. Cooper pedals up the long driveway to my house and right up over the grass to my bedroom window. And when I open the screen and climb in, Cooper behind me, everyone is there: Grandma, Grandfather, and Cat, staring into my closet.

Bloom has had her kittens.

# Chapter Ten

In the box of pictures, now ruined, were Bloom and her kittens: four tiny bodies, all wet and dark.

"I've only been gone an hour," I whispered.

Grandma smiled.

"That's all it takes, sometimes."

"Sorry about the pictures, Journey," said Grandfather.

I sighed.

"It's all right. It was impossible. But it was that baby's hand . . ." My voice trailed off.

We watched the kittens fumbling to nurse and listened to their soft mewings.

Bloom stared up at Grandma.

"Yes," Grandma said as if answering a question the rest of us hadn't heard, "you are a wonderful mother!"

Cat reached down and rubbed Bloom's chin.

"Who taught her?" I asked suddenly.

"Taught her what?" said Cooper. "How to have kittens?"

"No," I said. "How to be a mother."

There was a silence. Grandfather lifted his shoulders.

"Mothers know," he said, looking at Grandma.

Cat said what I was thinking.

"Not all of them."

No one spoke, but as if Bloom had understood our words, she began to clean her babies, showing us how to be a mother.

"Grandpa," I said, "I want to take a picture. With the timer."

My grandmother and Cat groaned at the same time.

"Oh, no," complained Cat. "Don't tell me, two of them!"

Grandfather grinned at me.

"Of course he wants to take a family picture. Out in the hall, Journey."

In the hallway Grandfather's camera and his tripod leaned against the wall.

"I'll take the picture. I'm not family," Cooper called to me.

I stood in the doorway and looked at Cooper through the viewfinder. His cowboy hat still sat on top of his head.

"Cooper," I said, "you're part of the family. But *I* want to take this picture."

When I moved the camera, I saw Grandfather smiling at me from across the room.

"Now," I said. "Everyone . . ."

There was laughter.

"What?" I asked.

"You sound like you-know-who," said Cat, bending her head toward Grandfather.

"Who?" asked Grandfather.

"The photographer twins," said Cooper wryly.

"Now," I said. "Everybody . . ." I shot a look at Cat.

Grandma sat, Cat next to her, leaning back against her shoulder. Cooper knelt behind them, Grandfather on the other side, watching me closely.

"Ready?" I said.

Time slows somehow as I look through the camera. I watch Bloom look at her babies; I watch Grandma kiss the top of Cat's head and Cat turn to smile up at her; I see Cooper with his dumb hat, and my grandfather, smiling at me because he knows I am looking at him.

*Smile,* I say to them, but I don't need to say it because they are all smiling. Real smiles, with their eyes, too. *Ten, nine, eight,* I say, and Cooper's hat tilts and Cat snorts with laughter. *Seven, six.* I run to get into the picture, and Grandfather reaches out a hand toward me. I tumble into his arms, across his lap, and he holds me there, looking a little surprised, as if I'm a newborn baby. I stare at the button on his shirt. Then I stare up at his face. *Quick,* he whispers to me, and I turn and look into the camera just as the shutter clicks and Cooper's hat falls down.

The kitchen was dark and cool and quiet. Cooper had stayed for dinner: chicken and mashed potatoes and peas.

"It's good to eat with people who don't have food on their faces," said Cooper seriously. He paused. "But I love Emmett."

"You do," agreed Grandma.

Grandfather, his chin leaning on his hand, looked at Cooper.

"You're a good brother," he said.

Under the table I felt a sudden brush against my legs. Bloom looked up at me; then she walked to the screen door.

"Where's she going?" I asked, alarmed.

Cat got up from the dinner table.

"She's going out, Journey. Don't fret." She opened the door, and Bloom went out to sit on the porch. Cat turned to look at me. "She'll come back," she said softly.

Cooper got up, too.

"Thank you," he said. "I like to get home for Emmett's bath."

He went out to the porch and stood for a moment next to Bloom. Then he put on his hat.

" 'Bye, Cooper," said Cat.

We went out, all of us, and waved to Cooper.

"Maybe someday," said Cat thoughtfully, "I *will* marry him."

Grandma, smiling, tapped Cat on her shoulder. The two of them went to their garden.

Grandfather stood next to me, fiddling with his camera. I looked up at him, trying hard to remember something new, something at the edge of my mind. He put the camera around his neck.

"Think I'll take a small walk to the henhouse."

I smiled and watched him walk down the steps. Inside, the phone rang, and he turned.

"I'll get it," I called to him.

"Hello."

I look out the screen door.

"Journey, is that you?" says my mother.

There is crackling on the line, and I stand very still, watching my grandfather walk away from the house.

"Journey?" Her voice is stronger now. "So, how have you been?"

I take a breath.

"A cat has come," I say. "And the cat is a very good mother." My voice rises. "And she is staying here with me. Forever."

# Chapter Eleven

Grandfather found me in the barn. Light slanted through the windows, and dust motes floated in the air between us. He sat next to me on the bench in front of the wall of pictures. There were dozens now that spread across the back wall, some I'd never seen.

"That's a new one," I said, pointing to a close-up of a fierce-looking chicken.

"That chicken pecked me on the wrist," said Grandfather. He held out his hand to show me the small red puncture wound. "Taking pictures is dangerous business."

I nodded, looking at the picture I had taken, all

soft and blurred. My grandfather holding Emmett on his knees.

There was silence.

"She asked me how I was," I said after a moment. I looked up at Grandfather. "And she never said she was sorry for leaving."

Grandfather sighed.

"No. Liddie doesn't want to feel guilty."

"Well, she is guilty," I said so softly that Grandfather bent his head down next to me to hear. "And then she said, 'They were only pictures, Journey.'"

Grandfather reached over and put his arm around me. I leaned against him.

"A picture stops a little piece of time, good or bad, and saves it," he said. "Your mama never thought there was anything worth looking back on after your papa left. She thought all good things were ahead of her, waiting to happen . . . just around the corner. Your mama doesn't really understand about the pictures."

"But we understand, don't we," I said.

Grandfather's arm tightened around me.

"We do."

I sighed.

"I sure would like things to look back on."

It was quiet in the barn. Somewhere in the garden Grandma was playing the flute, the beginnings of a song I didn't know.

"Grandma's getting better," I said.

"Yes," said Grandfather. "And it's a good thing, too," he added, making me smile.

"Mama wants me to visit her," I said.

Grandfather got up and went to the wall of pictures and bent down as if he were examining them.

"I told her I couldn't. I told her I have a cat and kittens to take care of."

Grandfather straightened.

"I told her someday, maybe; if she sent me words instead of money, I might visit. Maybe."

Grandfather said nothing.

"Grandfather?"

"What, Journey?" His voice was soft.

"I told her that nothing is perfect. Sometimes things are good enough."

I got up and stood next to him and looked at the family picture of all of us, our necks all white in the sun as we looked up at the airplane overhead.

"I like that picture," I said.

"So do I. You said it would be a good picture. Remember?"

I looked at the picture of us all framed in the barn doorway, with a blur of chicken flying past.

"Is that the chicken that pecked you?" I asked.

Grandfather began to laugh.

"Might be!"

He threw back his head, and I stared at him, surprised at that sound. It had been a long time since I'd heard him laugh, and suddenly I thought of Mr. MacDougal's kiss on my forehead, how strange it had felt.

I watched Grandfather. And then, before he stopped laughing—because I wanted to remember what it was like—I stood on tiptoe and kissed him.

# Chapter Twelve

Two months. Two months and a little more had gone by. It didn't seem so long when you said it, but Grandma said that time was different depending on which journey you were taking—a trip to the mountains or a trip to get your tooth pulled.

"Sometimes things happen quickly before you have a chance to think about them. Like the hummingbird that comes to my bee balm in the garden," said Grandma. "You don't see him come, and you hardly see him go."

Like Mama's leaving.

Two months. The kittens had grown what seemed half a lifetime in that time, staggering around the house, leaping straight up in the air when they came on Grandfather's boots. Emmett was learning words like "Mama" and "Da." Cooper was trying to teach him "disintegrate."

Grandma, in that time, had made it through an entire song, from beginning to end, on the flute. Vivaldi it was, she said.

"*My* version of Vivaldi," she added.

Grandfather made several trips to town in the car, alone, giving us all sly looks as he left and sly ones when he returned. He carried packages, and one large box, into the barn.

"Do not follow me!" he commanded in a loud, serious voice, making Cat and me burst out laughing and Grandma smile.

"What's he doing?" Cat asked Grandma.

"Secrets," said Grandma. "Secrets even from me, can you believe that?"

She walked to the entrance of the barn.

"Marcus, darlin' man," she called. "What are you doing?"

Grandfather's voice came from the back of the barn.

"Don't sweet talk me, Lottie."

Grandma went back to practicing Vivaldi on the

porch, surrounded by her claque of cats, and later, when my sister and I went to the barn for raspberry buckets, there was a shiny new lock on the door to the toolroom. Grandfather wasn't in sight, but we heard sounds behind the door.

Cat knocked.

"Grandfather?"

"I'm busy now." His voice was muffled. "I'm busy in my office."

His office? Cat mouthed the words to me, and we grinned at each other and went to pick black raspberries.

The raspberries grew past the pasture, at the far edges of the meadow where wild chicory and Queen Anne's lace grew, too. Grandma had put a net over them to keep the birds away. Cat and I pushed back the net and ducked under.

"Every third or every fourth?" Cat asked, holding a berry to her lips.

"Every other?"

"Third," Cat said, popping the berry into her mouth.

We picked for a while in silence. The berries made a soft plunking sound when we dropped them in the buckets.

"Remember when we used to make tents in the backyard?" I said, sitting back, looking up at the sky through the netting.

Cat nodded.

"You liked to build the tents," she said. "And when you were done you'd sit inside, all restless and jittery, waiting for something more to happen."

"That's because I loved to build them," I said.

"And I loved to sit inside after you'd gone," said Cat.

There was a silence. Cat reached over to touch my arm.

"What are you thinking about?"

"Something Grandfather said, Mama waiting for things to happen. Remember when Mama got into the tent with us once?"

Cat nodded.

"She sat for a minute, then looked at us and said, 'Well, what happens now?'"

"You and I," I said, "we weren't enough."

I ate a raspberry. It was sour, and for a moment my tongue stung a little.

"Cat."

She looked up.

"I'm sorry. I'm sorry I couldn't put the pictures together. I wanted to make things all right again."

Cat smiled.

"I know. You and Grandfather, two of a kind."

"What do you mean?"

Cat sat back on her heels.

"Why do you think Grandfather takes family pictures?"

"He likes to. He likes the camera."

"No," said Cat. "*You* like the camera in your own way, Journey. Don't you know that Grandfather wants to give you back everything that Mama took away? He wants to give you family."

All those times. All those times that Grandfather had rounded us up, gathered us together for family pictures; plucking us out of hiding places, down from trees and from inside the pantry and from under the bed.

"Things for me to look back on," I whispered.

"Things for him to look back on, too," Cat added.

Cat dropped a berry in the bucket.

"Cat, do you hate Mama?"

Cat stared at the bucket.

"I hate what she did."

I nodded.

"You say that, but do you feel that way?"

Cat looked up.

"I'm trying."

I squeezed a berry between my fingers.

"Do you think she cares about us?"

Cat sighed.

"The only way she can, Journey."

She ate a berry, and the juice made a tiny rivulet down her chin. I peered up suddenly at the sun shining through the net like an out-of-focus picture, then back at Cat. The pattern of the netting sat like a spider web across her face.

"What? What's wrong?" she asked me.

"I wish I had Grandfather's camera right now," I said, beginning to smile.

Cat's eyes widened. I got up quickly, and she scrambled up and after me, chasing me out into the meadow. We startled the redwings, and they flew up above us. A woodchuck on the stone wall ducked away.

Behind us the birds began to eat the raspberries under the net, but it didn't matter.

# Chapter Thirteen

It was evening, and the moon hung over the barn. Bloom lay on my bed. Upstairs, over my head in Mama's room, there were footsteps. Bloom looked up and her ears rose. A drawer opened and shut, then another. I looked up, waiting, and in a moment Grandfather stood at my bedroom door.

"Good night, Journey."

He held a large envelope and one of the kittens.

"Are you going to bed now?" I asked.

Grandfather, not speaking, stared over my head at the moon out the window. He had been restless and absentminded all day, drumming his fingers on the table at dinner, pursing his lips thoughtfully.

Twice he opened his mouth to say something and didn't. Once, in the middle of our conversation, he said suddenly, "Well, do you think . . . ?" to no one. We had turned to look at him, waiting, but he'd gone back to eating.

"He's cooking up something," Grandma had said at the kitchen sink, handing me a dish to dry. "I would spy on him, or better yet, ask him, but it's too much fun making him wait."

"You mean he wants to tell us what he's doing?"

"Maybe. Maybe he wants to be asked, but you can do that when the time comes."

"When? What time?"

"You'll know," Grandma had said.

Grandfather stood still in my bedroom. The kitten in his arms yawned.

"Grandfather. Grandfather?"

"What? Oh, no, I'm not going to bed yet." He shook his head. "No, I've got work to do."

He put the kitten down and looked at me with a small smile that was more than just a smile.

"Grandfather, were you in Mama's room?"

"Ah, yes. . . ."

I knew the tone. He didn't want to say, or he wouldn't say.

"The kitten had gone in there," he said. "Well, good night."

"Good night."

I heard his footsteps down the hallway and into the kitchen. Then the screen door opened and shut with a small squeak. Out my window I watched him cross the yard and go into the barn, shutting the door behind him. Inside, the barn light went on. Then, as I watched, it went off again.

*I am asleep and flying. Cooper and Emmett are there in my dream, and I patiently explain that this is a dream, my flying dream. Cooper smiles at me, and Emmett reaches out a small hand to touch me. "Do you think we could fly, too?" asks Cooper. I am about to say "yes," but I say "wait" instead.*

"Wait!" I said out loud.

I sat up in bed, awake. Beside me the kittens stirred. I got out of bed and walked to the window. The moon had gone, but the outside light was on. I turned the lamp on beside my bed. It was four o'clock. Bloom, from her box in the closet, made a small sound in her throat. I turned off the light and went down the hallway, barefoot, and out into the yard.

The moon had set behind the house. I picked my way across the yard, wishing I had thought of shoes. There was dew on the grass and on the stones when I got to the driveway. Very slowly I opened the barn door and slipped inside. I had never been in the barn at night, and there were new shapes and shadows. It did not look like the same place that it was in daylight. It was as if I were still dreaming, as if I had come to a different barn that was like but not like our barn.

I walked past the grain buckets and the wooden bins; somewhere behind the hay there was a rustle, a mouse or a barn rat. I walked past the stalls to the back of the barn. The door to Grandfather's back room was closed, but a slice of red light spilled across my bare toes through the space at the bottom of the door. Very carefully I turned the knob. Very slowly I pushed the door open.

The room was filled with the red light, spilling over the table, over equipment, over my grandfather. There was a sharp, strange smell in the room. Grandfather bent over a tray of liquid, staring at something there. Then he picked up a piece of paper out of the tray.

Grandfather set Grandma's metronome going, and it began to click back and forth. *Click. Click. Click.* I watched it, half hypnotized by the sound and the movement. And then, very slowly, Grandfather turned his head and looked at me. He looked at my pajamas, then down at my feet. *Click. Click. Click.*

"Where are your shoes?" he asked, his voice making me jump.

I opened my mouth to answer him, and then I saw it. Behind Grandfather, hanging on a line, held by clothespins, was my family picture. The picture of the kittens and Bloom in a box, Cooper with his cowboy hat, Cat leaning against Grandmother, and me, lying in Grandfather's arms, my face turned to the camera with a startled look.

"What . . ." I started to speak.

"Don't talk for a minute," said Grandfather, taking what I saw was a picture out of a tray and putting it into another.

He reached up and turned the red light out and the overhead light on. I blinked, then came closer to the table and looked down. It was the picture of

Cooper on his bicycle, his mouth open, looking amazed.

"The day I drove the car," I said.

Grandfather smiled at me.

"A darkroom," I said, smiling back at him. "You did this?"

Grandfather, his hair all tousled, grinned wider.

He saw me looking at my family picture.

"That is a fine picture," he said.

"Not perfect," I said. "But . . ."

"Good enough," we said, almost at the same time.

Then Grandfather lifted his shoulders in a sigh, his face slipping out of his grin.

"And there's more, Journey," he said softly.

In the large envelope are the negatives of Mama's pictures. Grandfather spreads them out on the table, and I hold one up to the light, my hand trembling. The people in the picture, all white as if they've been caught in a flash of sun, stare at me. There is a baby.

"This one," I say, my voice a whisper.

Grandfather nods and hands me another. He watches me as I hold it up.

It is a man, a baby on his knees. I stare at it for a moment. Then Grandfather reaches up to turn on the red light.

Grandfather talks softly all the time, his face touched by the glow of the red light, telling me what he's doing. But I hardly hear his words. He tells me about the enlarger and how it works, but silently I wait and watch as, like a face out of the fog, Mama's face appears on the paper, Papa beside her, the two of them smiling at the baby who is me. The baby's hand reaches out and the mother bends toward him. After the shutter clicks she will kiss him.

I stare at Mama's face. Then at Papa's. And something that I've been trying to remember appears in my mind suddenly, like a face on a piece of paper. My papa's face is a face I don't know. *It is a face I don't remember.*

Grandfather washes the picture and hangs it up to dry. He sucks in his breath with a little whooshing sound.

"Now," he says, "the other picture."

I put my hand on his arm.

"I know," I say. "I already know."

Grandfather is not surprised. He smiles a little and looks up at my family picture.

"I sat on *your* knees," I say, "not on Papa's. And you sang 'Trot, trot to Boston.' It was your shirt, your button I remembered." I pause, then whisper. "It was *your* face."

Grandfather takes down my family picture.

"And this was when you knew," Grandfather says.

I stare at my startled face in the picture as I lay sprawled in Grandfather's lap.

We turn out the lights and walk out into the barn. I trail my fingers along the wood walls. I touch the hay, as if touching it somehow makes it mine.

Grandfather reaches over and takes my hand. At the door I stop suddenly.

"Once they loved me," I say.

His hand tightens around mine, and when we open the door and walk out of the barn, the night has gone, and the sun has come up.

## ABOUT THE AUTHOR

Patricia MacLachlan won the 1986 Newbery Medal for *Sarah, Plain and Tall*. She and her husband, a psychologist, live in Williamsburg, Massachusetts. They have three grown children.